Clockwork Legion

By:

Jamie Sedgwick
Published by Timber Hill Press

Clockwork Legion
ISBN-13: 978-1540565969
Copyright 2016 by Jamie Sedgwick
Cover art copyright 2016 by Timber Hill Press
All Rights Reserved
This is a work of fiction. Any similarity to real events, people, or situations is coincidental.

Be sure to look for these other exciting titles:

Aboard the Great Iron Horse
steampunk series

The Tinkerer's Daughter trilogy
steampunk series

Hank Mossberg, Private Ogre
mystery/fantasy series

The Shadow Born Trilogy
YA fantasy/adventure

Karma Crossed
urban fantasy

The Darkling Wind
YA fantasy

Prologue

Engineer's Log

The jungle beyond Dragonwall is a world lost in time, populated by thousands of remarkable species and virtually untouched by modern civilization. Here, in the epicenter of one of the impact craters that nearly destroyed life on this planet, we have discovered a land teeming with it.

Upon our initial descent, we encountered a race of playful winged humanoids not much larger than doves. They were remarkably intelligent beings, if somewhat devious, and possessing limited speech capabilities. My crew called them "fairies" based upon their resemblance to the mythical creatures. While hovering overhead and eavesdropping on our conversations, these fairies picked up on a few words of our common tongue. Regrettably, they developed an immediate affinity for the worst sort of profanity -the exact sort at which my crew seems to excel- and I'm afraid the next explorers to encounter these delicate, fanciful creatures will be shocked by their uncomely utterances.

One additional note on these fairies: During our initial encounter, several landed on the rooftop and rails of the Iron Horse, and immediately dropped dead. A quick analysis of their corpses proved that their tiny bodies contained extremely high concentrations of starfall. Much like the dragons on the rim of the crater, these fairies have evolved not only to tolerate the effects of the element, but to *require* it in order to survive. The sudden leeching effects of the train's iron overwhelmed their delicate systems and killed them. So appears to be the situation with many of the beasts that populate the crater.

Our survey of the pools and deposits of starfall here has hindered our progress, as have our constant run-ins with numerous new and deadly species. It is at these moments that I become acutely aware of the dwindling numbers of my crew. The absence of Kale is particularly felt, along with Thane's long-time companion, Shayla. The pair were not only valuable crewmembers, but also close friends. I had been worried about the effect their absence might have. Thankfully, we all seem to be adjusting to the changes as well as can be expected. Suffice it to say that Kale's strong arm is missed, even if his brash temperament is not.

My cartographer Micah has been of immense help lately, spending most days atop the train, sketching his maps and drawings with exceptional skill. He's a fast worker, and conscientious, and thanks to his records, I can now say with a high degree of confidence that the starfall we have discovered in the crater should adequately power Sanctuary for at least a century. However, one cannot gauge with any certainty how the reserves will meet the needs of a rapidly expanding population, nor should one underestimate the challenges presented in extracting the fuel from this wild, unpredictable environment. For the moment, I remain hopeful.

Chapter 1

Socrates entered the Engineering car and found River gazing intently through one of the microscope lenses mounted on the tabletop. She leaned close to the lens, moving a small soldering iron back and forth, just outside his field of vision. As he gazed at her through his dark wire-rimmed glasses, Socrates heard a brief *hissing* noise, and a puff of smoke went up from the table. The acrid scent of burning rosin filled the room. The mechanical ape stepped closer, trying to get a glimpse of the project she was working on.

"Is there anything I can help you with?" he said in a deep rumbling voice.

River leaned back on the stool. She turned her head to stare at him, blinking as her eyes adjusted to the change in focus. Thin wisps of smoke curled up from the soldering iron still in her hand.

"What?" she said with a blank look. "Did you say something?"

Socrates chuckled, and his internal mechanisms made *clicking* noises as his shoulders shook. "I stopped in to check on an experiment," he said. "I didn't realize you would be working in here."

"Where else would I be?"

He gave her a weak smile. "Excellent point."

River had little interest in things outside of engineering. She was a wonderful mechanic -in fact, the train seemed to get better and better under her supervision- but Socrates was concerned about her relationships with the crew. "You really should get out of Engineering once in a while," he said. "Human contact is... important."

"If you say so," she said dismissively. River turned, and over her shoulder, Socrates caught a glimpse of what appeared to be a large metallic butterfly wing. He leaned closer. "What are you working on?"

River rotated the lens back toward the wall, moving it out of the way. She climbed off the stool, offering Socrates a clear view of her project. His simian features lifted as he stepped closer.

"A mechanical fairy?" he said. "River, it's ingenious! Tell me, how did you form the wings? You couldn't possibly have forged that brass by hand."

"I'm not giving away my trade secrets," River said.

Socrates reached for it and then paused, mid-movement. "May I touch it?"

"Of course. It's finished, but please be careful. It's very delicate."

"I can see that." The gorilla gently slid two massive fingers under the wings, and lifted the device for closer examination. He peered over the rims of his dark glasses. "Spring-loaded, double reverse hinges. Full-spread articulation. River, this design is absolutely brilliant. It might actually even fly!"

"Do you think?" she said with a sly grin. She took it from him, and Socrates watched in glee as River placed a key into a tiny hole in the fairy's back. She wound the internal spring, and after removing the key, pressed a hidden switch. A look of pure delight swept over the ape's features as the wings began to flap. They built up speed until they were a blur of brass and steel, and the gossamer fabric that made up the surface of the wings became all but invisible.

A gust of air hit Socrates in the face, like the wind from a tiny fan blowing back the midnight-blue fur on his cheeks, and the fairy took flight. It lifted horizontally from River's palm and rose several feet in the air. It hovered near the ceiling for a few seconds, and then zoomed over their heads, toward the far end of the room.

"Incredible!" Socrates exclaimed. "How do you control the creature's flight?"

"I've been meaning to talk to you about that. The controls are mechanical. I've programmed the dimensions of this room, so the fairy can fly back and forth without hitting the walls-" the fairy zoomed by, and River reached up to snatch it out of the air. "Unfortunately," she continued, "I haven't figured out a way to make it react with the environment. It's not intelligent. If an unmapped tree got in its way..."

"I see. So you want this creature to be semi-autonomous, then?"

"Sort of... something like a steamscout, I guess. I thought it would be a handy tool for surveying, possibly even for studying some of the species we've discovered, but without risking our lives."

"Agreed." Socrates folded his arms over his chest and tapped his chin with his forefinger. "I may have an idea. I've been studying some of the early steamscout technology. The more primitive versions were controlled using program cards; thin sheets with commands written into them using combinations of hole punches."

"Holes?"

"Yes, I know it sounds strange, but it's possible to store information this way. Think of the scroll in a music box or player piano. Reduced to its simplest form, all information is merely a switch that is on or off."

River blinked. "You've completely lost me. Anyway, that's why I wanted your help. Do you think you could come up with some sort of... punch card? A system of commands that could teach her to respond to her environment?"

"Perhaps," said the ape. "It would have to be very small. It would be limited by the amount of weight she could carry. And of course, multiple layers of commands would be necessary. Then there is the matter of recording information-"

A timer went off across the room, interrupting the ape. Socrates hurried over to the corner. River followed after him. Using a pair of tongs, the deep blue primate carefully removed a small pebble of ore from a glass vial. He placed it on the bench, and reached into an adjacent drawer, searching for his dyes.

"Is that iron?" River said, leaning over him.

"Yes... I've been trying to calculate the absorption rate of starfall into raw ore."

"Why?"

"As you know, starfall affects everything it comes into contact with, but it has a particularly unusual effect on ore." Socrates opened the vial of red dye and released a tiny drop onto the pebble. The dye ran in rivulets down to the tabletop, changing from red to violet as it touched the ore.

"What do you mean?"

"Do you understand what happens when a living creature -say a human- is subjected to high concentrations of starfall?"

"It alters her body," River said. "It changes her at a molecular level. Everybody knows that."

"Exactly. Hence the Tal'mar, the Vangars, the Kanters, and even our own cartographer. All of these races began, thousands of years ago, as humans." He paused to move the sample into a container. He dropped a spot of dye on the next ore sample, with the same results. As he worked, Socrates continued to explain:

"Obviously, stone is not living and cannot mutate in the way that other living creatures do. Starfall's reaction to the ore is entirely unique. The element somehow bonds with the ore at a molecular level, changing its properties in the process."

"Like Blackrock steel," River said. "In Astatia, where I grew up, the deposits of starfall in the Blackrock Mountains soaked into the ore. When forged into steel, it made unbelievably powerful springs. That's why my mother's planes were able to fly so far, and why she could rewind the springs by landing and taking off again."

"Yes, with diminishing returns of course, but nonetheless marvelous. The starfall stored in Blackrock ore made it somehow stronger and more energetic... and yet strangely stable."

"What do you mean?"

"A pebble of ore like this one," he said, holding it up with the tongs, "has absorbed the energy equivalent of a stick of dynamite. Yet we can put it in a fire and heat it. We can forge it into useful tools, or springs. I'm sure you're aware of what would happen to a stick of dynamite inside a forge, or under the pressure of a blacksmith's hammer."

"It would explode." River stared at the small black piece of metal. "So would starfall." Her eyebrows suddenly shot up. "You're saying starfall becomes *more* stable when it soaks into iron?"

"Precisely, but I don't know why, or if there is a tipping point. It may be that at certain levels, the iron is safe, while at higher concentrations it becomes unstable. Only a theory, of course. One which I have so far failed to prove."

The shriek of the Iron Horse's steam whistle interrupted their conversation. River tilted her head as she heard the sound. She stared at her companion curiously.

"Socrates... who is driving the train?"

The ape gave her a nervous smile. "Micah. It seemed safe enough. The train is only rolling at ten miles per-"

Before he could finish, the brakes locked up. The screech of metal against metal assaulted their ears, and the floor seemed to go out from under them. River fell backwards, landing flat on her back. She slid helplessly towards the front of the car as glass vials and tools crashed to the floor around her. Socrates fell sideways, tumbling as he threw his arms out in an attempt to catch himself. He slid after her, and they ended up in an awkward pile at the front of the car.

River grunted, trying to extricate herself from the tangle of arms, legs, and engineering tools. Socrates rolled aside, giving her the room to free herself. Micah's shrill voice came reverberating out of the communication pipes:

"Socrates! Socrates are you there? I need you!"

The couple leapt to their feet and dashed out the door.

Chapter 2

Kale tapped the heel of his boot against the kick-plate of his spring-powered horse, and it took a step to the right. The coil springs and pistons made a whining sound as the charger followed his command. The steel hooves *clacked* against the paving stones, and its ears perked up, almost as if it were a living creature. Kale knew that in reality, the ears were just sensors that helped maintain its balance and navigate through a complex landscape, but the effect was nonetheless convincing. In some ways, the mechanical charger behaved just like a real horse.

"It just doesn't *feel* like a regular horse," he mumbled. "It doesn't steer right."

Kale's companion, the aging knight known as Sir Gavin, snorted at the comparison. He ran a hand over the stubble of his close-cropped silver hair. "Few would know the difference," he said. "Real horses are rarer than diamonds in these parts."

Gavin's voice was deep and gravelly, possibly due to the bright red scar across his throat. Kale had a few scars of his own, not the least of which was the large red patch on his cheek that had been there since childhood. His were not as numerous as Gavin's perhaps, but Kale was less than half the elder knight's age. Gavin was in his sixties; the oldest of the knights at Dragonwall, and also one of the keep's oldest inhabitants. Kale had learned that men did not tend to grow to a ripe old age in Dragonwall.

That might change now, he thought. *Now that the black dragon is dead...*

"There must have been horses before," Kale said. "I've seen them in Dragonwall's tapestries. What happened to them?"

"Dragons, of course. That was long before my time, but my ancestors had a devil of a time keeping any livestock until they figured out how to camouflage their corrals. The serpents scattered the herds, driving them down with fire and then snatching them up into the air. Even now, we can't keep many around. Good thing we have plenty of dragons to eat."

Kale wrinkled up his nose. "I don't know how much more dragon I care to eat," he said. "I'd kill for some chicken, or a slab of beef."

Sir Gavin let out a hearty laugh. "I know a butcher on the outskirts of Stormwatch. I'll see what I can do. A few bites of meat shouldn't be too much to ask for the queens' First Knight."

They reached the gates to Dragonwall on the plateau overlooking Stormwatch. Kale dismounted and handed the care of his spring-powered mount to one of the guards. Sir Gavin followed after him.

As they entered the long stone passageway, a page came running up to them. He was only twelve years old, but already had the broad shoulders and bulging biceps that were so common of the men in Dragonwall. The people here weren't particularly tall, but they were strong from learning to work the forges as soon as they could walk. Even the women were just as comfortable swinging a hammer as rocking a cradle.

"Sir Kale," the page said breathlessly. "The queen requests your presence in her chambers immediately."

Kale frowned. "Is something wrong?"

"I don't know sir, she didn't say."

Sir Gavin nudged him. "Bet I know what's wrong," he said with a sly grin. "The queen must he getting lonely up at the top of the mountain, without a man there to take care of her."

Kale ignored the jab. The other knights had been teasing him about his close relationship with Queen Aileen almost since they day she'd knighted him, which was not long after her husband's death. There had been no shortage of whispering on that account, either.

Kale chose to turn a deaf ear to their conspiracies. Though he had only known King Dane a short time, he had considered the king a great friend, perhaps even a father figure. Kale missed Dane, and he felt an overwhelming sense of compassion for the widowed queen and her twin daughters. Perhaps even guilt. Since Dane's murder, not a day had passed that Kale hadn't wondered about whether he might have been able to save the king. *If only he had been faster... if only he had paid more attention...*

Dane's tragic and sudden death left the kingdom in a lurch. When Dane died, the power of the monarchy passed to his wife, a situation not without precedent, but this arrangement had always been considered temporary. According to custom, Aileen was supposed to choose the next king by marriage. Since Dane's death, the weeks had stretched into months, and still Aileen had given no indication of a prospective replacement for her spouse. Other than Kale, of course. His frequent visits to her chambers were completely platonic, but the busy minds and wagging tongues inside Dragonwall had their own ideas on the matter. The queen was in mourning, and had every right to be, but the people were growing impatient.

Kale entered the queen's apartment a few minutes later. He didn't bother knocking. The two were familiar enough that Aileen knew better than to expect much in the way of courtly manners from Kale. Besides, she had requested his presence. It wouldn't make much sense to summon him and then be surprised when he actually arrived.

When Kale burst through the door, he was surprised to find that Aileen wasn't alone. She sat on the sofa near the veranda, the sun shining in behind her, casting a warm glow about the room. Next to her stood Sir Lyndon, Aileen's personal advisor. He was a heavyset, mostly bald man who wore the elegant robes of a noble but had the demeanor of a spoiled prince. Though technically still a knight, he had retired from anything resembling real work.

Lyndon glanced disapprovingly as Kale entered the room, and then quickly drew his gaze back to the queen. Aileen said something to him in a low tone and then dismissed him. Lyndon gave her a slight bow before leaving. He made every effort not to look Kale in the eyes on his way out. When the door had closed, Kale approached the queen. She beckoned to him, and gestured for Kale to have a seat in the armchair across from her.

Aileen straightened the chestnut brown fabric of her dress. The forest green trim set off the queen's emerald eyes and her auburn hair fell around her shoulders, glinting in the morning sun. For a woman ten years his elder, Kale observed that she couldn't possibly have been more beautiful. The warrior perched himself on the edge of the seat cushion, leaning forward to face her with his elbows resting on his knees.

"I'm afraid Sir Lyndon has bad news," the queen said

"Does Sir Lyndon bring any other kind of news?" Kale said with a sneer.

A gentle smiled turned up the corners of her mouth. "I trust him," Aileen said. "He has long been a friend to my family."

"If he's so trustworthy, why won't he look me in the eyes, except when I catch him glaring at me from across the dining hall? He slinks around in the shadows of Dragonwall like a thief."

Aileen leaned closer, touching his hand. "My friend, do you not understand that some men are intimidated by you?"

Kale laughed.

"You may not believe it," she said, leaning back, "but it is true. You're tall and strong. You're handsome, and you are fearless. When you walk into the room, other men notice, whether you realize it or not. They react to you."

Kale rolled his eyes. "What favor do you want from me this time? It must be a big one."

Aileen's smile widened, and a mischievous sparkle came into her eyes. She almost said something, and then bit her tongue. The smile vanished:

"Kale, we have something serious to talk about. Another body has been discovered."

Kale closed his eyes and began massaging his eyelids with his thumb and forefinger. "Like the others?" he said.

"Yes, poisoned, sometime in the night. The killer dragged the body into a dark corner where it wouldn't be found until morning. I'm sure you are aware that this is the third poisoning inside Dragonwall since your arrival. People are beginning to talk."

"I can see why," Kale said. "I'll look into it."

"See that you do." She spoke in a voice that at once reminded him she was his queen, and also implied that she might know more about the subject than she let on. Kale cleared his throat as he rose to his feet.

"If there's nothing else-"

"There is, actually." Aileen lifted a sheet of parchment from the table. Kale accepted the document and looked it over. The scribblings were practically indecipherable. It didn't help that he wasn't much of a reader. He had learned the basics as a child, but rarely found the opportunity or desire to use the skill in his adult life. The letter was addressed to "Her Royal Highness," and signed by someone called Mayor Thom Bromwyl. Kale picked out a few words here and there -something about mutilated livestock and something else about defiled corpses- but none of it made any sense.

"What is it?" he said, handing it back to her.

"A request for reinforcements. Ravenwood is a village on the southwestern border, on the outskirts of our kingdom. We used to send patrols through the area, but over the last few years, our resources have gone entirely into staving off the dragons. According to that message, Mayor Bromwyl is deeply concerned about the safety of his community."

"Safety from what?"

"He doesn't say," she said with a distant look.

"Do you think it's dragons?"

"Perhaps. The dragon population has fallen since the death of the black. It may be that some of the creatures have migrated farther inland. That would be strange, though. It's not like them to go into the deep woods. They're large. They prefer wide open hunting grounds."

"I'm not sure what I can do," Kale said. "I have less than two dozen knights, and we need every one of them. We can't pull men out of the militia. We have too few fighting men as it is. It's going to take months to finish rebuilding Stormwatch. If dragons were to attack, or-"

"Yes, I'm all too aware of this," she said, waving off his concerns. She gazed into the fireplace with a distant look "In a way, I miss the dragons. They were our one true defense against foreign invaders. No one had any interest in invading Danaise with so many dragons here. Now that the population has fallen, word is bound to spread beyond our borders. I suppose it's only a matter of time before someone decides to test our defenses,"

"Not only that," Kale said. "I don't think you understand how valuable your resources are."

"Starfall," Aileen said, her voice nearly a whisper. She turned her head to gaze up into his face. "That's what you mean, isn't it? So strange that we've gotten by without it for all these centuries and yet it is the very lifeblood of this world. I suppose we must make preparations for the inevitable." She gazed into his eyes, taking his hands in hers. "Kale, do you believe your friends in this city of Sanctuary will trade fairly with us?"

"I think so," he said. "They need starfall, but they have valuable technologies to trade. They have airships unlike anything you've ever seen. And other things, too. Weapons, for example."

"Yes, I know. That is what worries me."

Kale frowned. "What do you mean?"

"If I'm to believe the stories you've told me about Sanctuary and Astatia, it hardly seems they have any reason to negotiate with us. They have the power to come and take whatever they want."

"They wouldn't do that."

"Are you so certain?"

Kale couldn't answer, and Aileen fell back into the sofa.

"Enough of these matters for now," she said, letting out a sigh. "I would like you to take a small detachment to Ravenwood. Patrol our border for a few days. If there is a threat growing in the west, I want to know about it."

"And the southern border?"

She dismissed the idea with a wave of her hand. "Ashago is known to the peasants as the Firelands. It is a place of nothing but ash and lava."

Kale nodded, and headed for the door. She called after him, "Oh, and one more thing: You and I have something important to discuss when you return."

Kale stepped out into the hall and pulled the door shut behind him. He took a moment to gather his thoughts. He knew what Aileen wanted to discuss, but he didn't even want to think about it. As he stood there, a woman's voice whispered out of the shadows, speaking his thoughts:

"Did she propose to you?"

Kale stared into the darkened hallway. The shapely figure of a young woman in a long crimson skirts came around the corner. She pulled the hood of her cloak back, revealing curled auburn hair and flawless olive skin. Her eyes were dark, her lips pouty and glistening with red lip paint. She moved with the graceful elegance of a swan.

"Shayla," Kale said, catching her by the arm. "Just who I wanted to talk to."

She gasped as he pulled her down the hallway and yanked her around the corner. He spun Shayla around, pressing her back up to the wall, and leaned in to kiss her. Her breath was hot and smelled like cinnamon, and Kale inhaled her scent as he pressed his lips towards hers. Suddenly, he felt the blade of a stiletto at his throat. His eyes widened.

"Be careful," she said. "I can be a very dangerous woman."

"I know," he said, forcing his lips closer. The blade tightened against his throat, punctured the skin like a pinprick, but he refused to give way. A drop of blood ran down his throat as he pressed his mouth tight against hers. Shayla struggled for a moment before giving in.

The blade disappeared, and her hand closed on the back of his neck, pulling him in tighter. For a few seconds, the world around them seemed to vanish. Her mouth was hot, her body soft and willing against his hardened muscles. His arm snaked around her, pulling her tight against him, squeezing her hard enough to lift her feet from the ground.

He pulled away. He stared smugly down at Shayla as she struggled to catch her breath. A hand went to her breast, and she licked her lips.

"That was not... nice," she panted.

"I thought it was." Kale tightened his grip on her, pulling her body tight against his. "I'm pretty sure you thought it was, too."

Shayla averted her gaze. "She won't quit, you know. Aileen won't stop until you agree to marry her."

"I don't want to marry her."

"You don't want to marry *anyone*," Shayla said with a disgusted look. "That's the problem with you. You're like a child in a playground, and the rest of us... we're all just toys to you."

"That's not true."

"It won't be for long, if you don't do something about the queen."

"Forget her," he said, leaning in for another kiss. Shayla pushed him away.

"Kale! This is not a game. This is something you need to take seriously." She glanced around, shocked by the volume of her own voice. Shayla lowered her tone to a whisper: "There are rumblings. These people... they don't trust a woman to rule over them. I'm afraid that something bad is going to happen soon."

Kale pulled back, frowning down at her. "Are you saying I *should* marry the queen?"

"Of course not!" She turned away, began strolling down the hall. Kale fell in next to her. "But someone has to... and I don't see who else that could be. The other men here are *unqualified,* to put it kindly. But I can tell you this: If you care about her at all, you must do *something,* and do it sooner rather than later."

"Why?"

"Because if you don't, Aileen will be banished. Maybe worse."

He froze mid-step and stared after her. Shayla continued walking. "How do you know that?"

"Because while you've been busy playing knights and dragons, I've been studying these people. Their culture is far more complicated than you realize. Do you remember when Dane threw that man into the lava for trying to rape me?"

"Of course. I'll never forget it."

"That's why he did it. These people... they *need* a leader like that. They need someone who will take decisive steps, who will act fearlessly, and if necessary, brutally to maintain order. Believe it or not, it makes them feel safe."

She had paused a few yards down the hall, and Kale hurried to catch up to her. "What do you think I should do?"

"I have no idea. But you'd better think of something."

They reached the intersection of the main tunnel, and as they stepped out onto the walkway, a workman in a spring-powered metal suit went stomping by carrying a pallet of wagon parts. A rush of warm air washed over them. It smelled of sulfur and burning iron. Wisps of smoke and steam curled up through the center of the mountain, racing towards the peak of the cone.

"I have to go," Kale said. "Before I leave, I have to ask you something. Did you have anything to do with the body they found this morning?"

Shayla stared at him, her face a mask of indifference. When she refused to answer, Kale grew irritated.

"Don't do it again," he said.

"It wasn't me. What do you think I am? Do you honestly believe I stayed here just so I could go around poisoning them all to death, one at a time?"

"You must have had something to do with it. You can't make me believe otherwise."

Shayla gave him a guilty smile. "If I had anything to do with it, it was only in giving these women the power to defend themselves. They have that right, whether you like it or not."

"That doesn't justify three killings in a row! This has to stop."

"How do you propose I do that?" she said. "The genie is out of the bottle, Kale. They have the knowledge. There is no way I can take that back."

"You'd better figure out a way, because if these killings don't stop, something bad *is* going to happen."

"That's the whole point."

Kale glared at her. "What is that supposed to mean?"

"This behavior, this raping and abusing... it's *going* to stop, one way or another."

"Poisoning every man in Dragonwall is not the answer," he said. "There's got to be another way."

"I'm sure there is. You're their commander. Figure it out."

Kale crossed his arms over his chest. "And just how do you propose I do that?"

"I don't know, but I can tell you one thing: If Dane was still alive, he would know. That man you found this morning wouldn't have been poisoned, he'd be frying in that lava pit."

She spun on her heels and hurried up the hall. Kale stared after her, watching until she disappeared around the corner.

Kale located Sir Gavin in the lower level of the mountain, overseeing the forge workers. The knight stood on the island, surrounded by a lake of boiling lava. Despite the heat of the volcano, Gavin was still dressed in full armor. His helm and gauntlets rested on a workbench nearby. Kale whistled to get Gavin's attention, and the elderly man hurried over to see what was the matter. Kale quickly explained the situation with Ravenwood.

"It won't be a standard patrol," Kale said. "It will be a reconnaissance mission. I'd like you to go with me. You know the border lands better than anyone."

"Of course," Gavin said, wiping the sweat from his brow with a strip of cloth. "We can be in Ravenwood before nightfall. We can spend the night there, before moving on."

"My thoughts exactly. I figured five men in total would be enough. Do you have any suggestions?"

Gavin considered for a moment. "We might be better off alone. The knights have been drinking. I doubt they'll be much use."

"It's ten o'clock in the morning."

"What's that got to do with anything?"

Kale took a deep breath. "Did King Dane have this sort of discipline problem?"

"No, but that was Dane. Don't hold yourself to that standard, boy. You'll just end up getting yourself killed."

Kale frowned. "What do you mean?"

"Dane knew these men. They were his kin; his childhood friends. He knew that when push came to shove, they would be there for him. For you, it's different. You're an outsider."

"But I'm still their commander."

"That, and three coppers will buy you breakfast at a nice restaurant in Stormwatch."

"Three coppers will buy anyone breakfast."

"Exactly," Gavin said. He clapped his hand down on Kale's shoulder and laughed. Kale shook his head.

"How do I make them respect me?"

"I can't tell you that, but I can tell you how Dane did it."

"How?"

"He threatened to kill 'em, or worse. And they knew he meant it. But that only worked because they *knew* Dane had the guts to do what he said, and *he knew* they didn't have the guts to stab him in his sleep."

"And you think that's what I should do?"

"Absolutely not! These men wouldn't hesitate to kill you in your sleep."

Gavin grinned as he said it, but there was a serious look in his eyes. Kale knew the old knight well enough to know he was trying to make light of a serious situation.

"You're not much help," Kale said. "I thought people your age were supposed to be wise."

"I am wise. Wise enough to avoid a knife between my shoulder blades. Are you?"

Kale snorted. "We're wasting time. Where can I find the others?"

"In the barracks."

Kale left Gavin with the orders to prep supplies for their journey. He headed upstairs to the barracks. When he arrived, he found the place in a shambles. A gut-wrenching smell of yeast and sewer washed over him as he stepped into the room, and Kale had to clench his teeth to fight back the urge to vomit.

Dirty dishes, unwashed clothes, and overflowing chamber pots littered the floor. Even Kale, who was not by any stretch the cleanest man, was disgusted. Some of the men were asleep, stretched awkwardly across their bunks or collapsed in heaps on the floor. A group sat at a card table at the end of the room, drinking and playing.

"Gentlemen," Kale said in a loud voice as he approached. One or two glanced at him, and then went back to their cards. The others ignored him entirely. Kale passed one of the bunks where a half-dressed knight was snoring. He grabbed the man by the ankle and yanked him out of bed. The knight dropped to the floor with a groan. He rolled over, both hands squeezeing his skull, moaning about his "achin' brainpan."

"I need three volunteers," Kale said as he reached the table.

The men ignored him, and continued playing. As they finished their hand, one of the younger knights named Sir Flynn reached for the pot. He was in his early twenties; a strong and arrogant young man with the physical prowess to be a knight, but very little experience. Kale caught him by the wrist, causing the coins to scatter across the table.

"You just volunteered," he said. "Get suited up and meet me out front in ten minutes."

Flynn yanked his hand away. He pushed to his feet, kicking his chair out behind him. "What if I don't want to *volunteer?*" he said, his lip curling up in a snarl. "What if none of us want to?"

Kale straightened up, looking them in the eyes one by one. Each looked away, or avoided his gaze entirely, except for Flynn. The young knight glared at him, defiant, challenging. Kale reached over the table in a flash of movement and caught the front of Flynn's shirt. With a snarl, he dragged the knight over the table. Cards and coins scattered, and the other knights scrambled to get out of the way as the table collapsed.

Kale spun, using his momentum as he turned, and threw Flynn across the room. The knight landed on his side and rolled a few turns across the stone floor before he caught himself. Flynn's hand went to his boot, and Kale saw the glint of his stiletto blade as Flynn leapt to his feet. Flynn rushed him.

Kale bent over, snatching up one of the broken table legs. As Flynn came at him, the commander stepped aside. He brought the wooden leg upward, driving it into Flynn's gut. As the knight stumbled, Kale brought it down with a *crack!* across his back. Flynn fell, toppling down on top of the broken table. He gasped, struggling to catch his breath.

Kale tossed the table leg aside and bent over him. He took the dagger from Flynn's hand. "Now," he said. "Anyone else care to volunteer?"

There was a shadow in the corner of his eye, but Kale couldn't react before the cold blade of a dagger touched his throat.

"I think it's time for you to leave," said a hoarse voice. Kale recognized it as Sir Bane. He glanced around the room. The sleeping knights had begun to rouse themselves to observe the fight. Those who had been playing cards stood back, watching. Flynn, somewhat recovered now, crawled to his feet.

Kale threw his head back, smashing the back of his skull into Bane's face. The middle-aged knight fell back, crying out as blood gushed from his broken nose. He dropped to his knees and went scrambling back, away from the fight.

Flynn took a step in Kale's direction. Kale's arms swung in a blur, and the stiletto flew past Flynn's face, barely grazing his cheek. It thudded into the wooden post behind him.

Flynn snarled. He took a step closer, his arm raised to strike. Kale stepped inside the swing and brought his fist up, driving it into Flynn's jaw. The young knight stumbled back.

Kale advanced, taking a second swing. This time, his left hand connected solidly with Flynn's forehead. The young knight dropped like a sack of rocks. He crumpled, landing on top of a sleeping knight, and lay there with his head lolling back. Flynn didn't move. Kale stared down at him a moment. Once he was certain the fight was over, he raised his gaze and found the other knights glaring at him.

"Well?" he shouted. "Who's coming with me?"

They all rushed him at once.

Chapter 3

Micah was in a nervous panic. The halfling paced back and forth across the locomotive platform, in and out of the cab, leaning over the rail now and then to peer out into the jungle. What he saw there sent shivers crawling up and down his spine. He was tempted to open the communication pipe again and find out what was taking Socrates so long.

As he spun around for the tenth time, Socrates and River burst through the door of the tender car and onto the platform. Micah let out a gasp, and stumbled back against the wall with his hands on his heart. His wide-brimmed hat fell down over his eyes.

"What's going on?" River demanded, staring down at him like a scolding mother with her hands on her hips. "Why did you hit the brakes?"

"Devils, don't do that!" Micah said, adjusting his hat. The long colorful feather sticking out of the hatband brushed against the wall behind him. "You nearly stopped my heart."

River glared at him. "Micah, you can't just-"

Micah put his finger to his lips in a *shushing* gesture. He poked his head around the corner of the cab. River leaned around behind him and her jaw dropped as she saw the cause of their sudden stop.

Down the embankment to their left, less than fifty yards from the track, was an exact replica of the Iron Horse. Just like the Horse, it was at least twice the size of an ordinary train, requiring a double set of tracks.

Each rail car was approximately the size of a small two-story house. There were only a dozen cars however, and the last few were lying on their sides at the end of the train. The locomotive at the front was tilted precariously, with the broken railroad tracks projecting up out of the undergrowth in front of it.

"What does it mean?" River said under her breath. Socrates shifted, and she became aware of the ape's presence next to her. His stiff blue fur grazed her arm and something inside of him made a quiet *whirring* noise.

"I don't know," the steam-powered gorilla said in a low, quiet voice. "I can only guess this train originated in Sanctuary. It must have been here for centuries."

"What happened to it?" Micah said. Socrates glanced down at him. The tiny exhaust chimney behind the ape's ear glimmered in the sunlight.

"It appears this train derailed, or at least that that the tracks were damaged. I wonder whether the builders ever learned of its fate."

"There are more tracks?" said Micah. "What for?"

"They're old," said River. "The steamscouts must have laid new tracks around the crash site." She narrowed her eyes as she stared at the ancient vehicle. "Socrates, I think somebody's in there."

They all stared. Here and there, every few seconds, they caught a glimpse of a shadow moving behind the foggy, mildew-covered glass.

"Who could it be?" Micah said.

River shrugged. "Could be animals. Or maybe someone discovered the train and turned it into a shelter."

"Or maybe they're hiding," Socrates said, nodding his head. River followed his gaze. Her eyebrows narrowed as she saw a massive reptilian creature lurking in the woods beyond the wrecked train. It was easily thirty feet tall and twice that length from snout to tail. It stood upright on its hind legs, the two forelegs strangely undeveloped for its size, the long serpent-like tail trailing out into the jungle.

"Socrates, there's something strange about that dragon."

"It doesn't have wings," Micah said helpfully.

"It's not a dragon," Socrates said. "It's called a dinosaur... or, at least that's what humans called its ancient ancestor. The original dinosaurs were already extinct when humans discovered their bones. Over the centuries, they developed numerous theories about the origins and extinction of these creatures. Most records of that time are lost, but I have numerous references in my memory banks, if you'd like to hear them."

"Maybe later," River said. "Socrates, do you see what I see?"

"Yes," the ape said matter-of-factly. "This creature is dead. Or perhaps I should say undead."

Micah's eyes doubled in size. "You mean-"

"Yes, it's like the Ancients in Blackstone Castle. The beast must have died weeks ago, judging by the looks of it, but the starfall in its brain remains active. I must admit, I'm not surprised. With the prevalence of starfall in this environment, I had expected to see more of this phenomenon. Frankly, that's one reason I've been loathe to stop the train unless it's absolutely necessary."

Micah concealed his face in his hands. "This is all my fault," he said in a muffled voice. "I never should have pulled the brakes."

Socrates put a comforting hand on his shoulder. "You did no wrong, Micah. This missing train might provide valuable insights into our history."

The halfling's face went pale. "You don't mean we're staying here? It's not safe! We should go..." He took a step toward the train's controls. "I'll just release the brakes, and-"

"We can't leave," River said. "What if someone is trapped inside that train?"

Micah glanced back and forth between them. His face fell as he realized they weren't going to change their minds.

"It wouldn't be conscionable to proceed without further investigation," Socrates said. "Likewise, we may find useful supplies on that train. At the very least, I would like to locate the Engineer's log and ascertain what exactly happened here."

"What about the... the dinosaur?"

"We'll have to wait for it to wander off," said River.

"That may not be an option," Socrates said, scratching his chin. "Do you see the way he's been watching us?"

River nodded.

"If you recall, the previous undead creatures we encountered had a certain... *predilection* for the living."

Micah gulped. "You mean he wants to eat us?"

"Not me," said Socrates with a wry grin. "I'm a machine. But I'm sure he would *love* to eat you."

Micah's glare said he didn't appreciate the ape's humor.

The undead dinosaur, apparently intrigued by the Iron Horse, took a few steps closer. Micah backed across the platform, reaching for the door of the tender car. "I think we should get inside," he said in a quivering voice.

"Indeed," said Socrates. "River, what weapons do we have that can kill a creature that size?"

"Are you kidding?" she said.

"What about our muskets?"

"Scatterguns and flintlocks," she said. "Nothing larger than fifty caliber. That would hardly penetrate the scales. I wish we had the *bonecrusher* right now."

Socrates turned and gestured that they should go inside. As they began to move, the dinosaur broke into a run. It flew across the clearing and leapt up the hill in three strides, but by this time, the adventurers were already safely inside. That did not deter the beast. The creature's massive jaws closed around the brass handrail at the front of the first passenger car and it began shaking left and right. The metal shrieked and bent, but held fast.

Undeterred, the undead dinosaur moved around to the broadside of the car, where it hauled back and rammed its massive head against the framework. The passenger car shook, the heavy steel chassis squeaking as it rocked back and forth. One of the windows cracked, but otherwise the damage remained minimal.

Socrates and River were already several cars down, casually discussing the situation as they moved deeper into the Horse. Micah had gone ahead to warn the others not to leave the train.

"If we had a cannon," River said, "we might be able to mount it on a steamscout. But it would take a few hours to manufacture something big enough to hurt him. That is, assuming we have a hardened steel pipe large enough."

"No, that's no good," said Socrates. "There's no framework to mount a cannon. Besides, it wouldn't be very useful in this terrain. The steamscouts are slow, lumbering machines."

As they wandered down the passageway, the undead beast finally gave up on trying to flip the car. It circled the front of the train, looking for signs of movement, unaware for the moment that its prey had already progressed deep into the bowels of the train.

*

Several hours later, Socrates and his crew were still trapped inside the Horse, and they had yet to develop a plan to deal with the creature. The zombie-like beast was determined to find a weakness in the train's design. It hadn't figured out about doors and windows yet, but River feared that it would learn soon enough. It had spent the entire morning clawing, biting, and ramming various sections of the train.

Frustrated with their lack of progress, River approached Socrates with a plan he had already rejected once:

"The *boneshaker* is perfect for this job," she said. "With only two wheels, it's narrow enough to move between the trees and undergrowth, and it's faster than any animal could ever run. I'll be fine. I'll draw it away, and then circle back once I've lost it."

Socrates had to concede that this seemed to be their only option. "Foolhardy as your suggestion is, I can't think of any other way to clear our path to the wreck. The more time we waste, the greater the danger... I'm concerned that if we don't get moving soon, that creature will eventually damage the Iron Horse."

"Then let me go!" she pleaded. "I can do this."

Socrates sighed. "I'll gather a boarding party and arm them with muskets. Please, be careful."

River was gone in a flash. She hurried down the passages, past Engineering and her bunkhouse, over a quarter mile to the railcar where she kept her *boneshaker*. It had been months since she'd used the steam-powered bike, but when she pulled the canvas away, the brass still gleamed like new.

A large cobweb dangled from the handlebars, and another stretched across the lower part of the holding tank and the engine. River wiped the webs away with a greasy rag. She hurried to fill the tank with fresh water, and when that task had been completed, she carefully lowered a small vial of diluted starfall into the fuel chamber. The trickle of flames from the old fuel instantly ignited the new supply. River closed the burner. While the tank heated, she returned to her bunkroom for a few necessities.

The room was dark when River entered, save for the pale light streaming in from the hall. She took a moment to open the drapes on the outer wall. The narrow shafts of light cutting through the canopy of trees illuminated the small space, revealing a single brass bed, a dresser, a washroom, and very little else.

The place was stark, but familiar and comfortable in its own way. River was a woman of few material possessions. Her one great treasure was the spring-powered revolver she had inherited from her mother. She took it from the hook on the wall and strapped the gun belt around her hips. River checked the firearm to be sure it was loaded and the spring was wound.

Satisfied, she holstered the weapon and turned to retrieve her bullwhip hanging in a coil by a second hook. She slung it through the small metal loop on her belt.

River headed back to the bike. By the time she had returned, the *boneshaker* was ready to go. Through the communication pipes, she informed Socrates that she was about to leave. She unlatched the door on the boxcar wall and shoved it aside with a loud rattling noise. There was no way to do this quietly or inconspicuously, but that didn't matter: River wanted the beast's attention.

River straddled the boneshaker, revved up the throttle, and kicked it into gear. The rear tired shrieked as it burned into the wood floor. It suddenly caught traction, and the bike leapt through the door. The cool, humid air washed over River. Her long blonde hair flew wild in the breeze. A world of deep green foliage spread out before her. There was a moment of almost perfect silence, and then the boneshaker landed with a *whomp!* The chassis squeaked and rattled, and the rear tire bit into the soft ground, throwing a spray mud and rocks into the air.

A few hundred yards to her right, the massive reptilian beast raised its head and fixed its gaze on her. River hit the brakes and slid into a sharp turn. The rear end swung around and she came to a stop alongside the train, halfway down the slope, facing the dinosaur.

For a moment, they just watched each other. The creature tilted its head from side to side, staring at her curiously. River twisted the throttle and made a beeline for it. The boneshaker surged forward, crashing through the ferns and bushes. Branches slapped at River's face and arms. She had forgotten her goggles, but it was too late to turn back now. She had the creature's full attention. The dinosaur threw its head back and roared. She saw the glimmer of intelligence in the creature's dull blue eyes. Those eyes were dead, no doubt about it, the frozen eyes of a stiff corpse watching her from afar. And yet it wasn't dead.

Not dead enough, River thought.

A few yards from the creature, River turned aside and shot down the embankment adjacent to the abandoned train. The dinosaur snapped at her as she swooped past, but River was safely out of reach. She straightened her course, shooting past the wrecked locomotive, and heading down the old tracks. The dinosaur broke into a run, snarling and slavering as it went bounding after her.

The boneshaker rattled beneath her, the front tire bouncing erratically across the uneven terrain. Even with the modification of added springs to the seat, the machine still seemed determined to shake River's teeth out of her skull. She gripped the handlebars and dared a glance over her shoulder. The dinosaur was just a few steps behind, snapping at her like a rabid dog.

River dodged left and right as the ferns and branches slapped at her face. The boneshaker careened, lurching, vibrating, shaking beneath her. The land rose and fell, and River found herself speeding down a narrow incline towards a stream. The boneshaker briefly took flight and then landed with a heavy *thud* at the bottom of the hill. Water splashed up, spraying her face, soaking her clothes.

The *boneshaker's* front tire rebounded off the rocks like a trampoline. River almost lost control as the handlebars shook. She clenched her teeth, leaned into the bars, and headed up the embankment. As she turned to follow the trail at the crest of the hill, the pursuing monster leapt from the other side of the stream. It cleared the ravine in a single leap and landed heavily just behind her. River wound the throttle up as tight as it would go.

The woods around her became a blur. The ferns and plant life melded into a wall of green. Shafts of sunlight slanted down through the trees, flashing in her eyes like the beam of a crude electric lamp flickering on and off. Vines dangled down from the trees. Shadowy figures moved here and there among the canopy. The entire world seemed to close in around her, forming one long, narrow tunnel.

The flashing light seemed to blind her. The wind was loud in her ears, the dinosaur behind her almost forgotten as the engine roared between her legs. Up ahead, the trail seemed to level out. Suddenly, the world opened up: The trees vanished. The ground disappeared. River shot over the edge of a cliff, and found herself plummeting into a vast ravine.

Four hundred feet below, sunlight glistened on the murky green waters of a river. Tree branches stretched out overhead, vines hanging down, ferns up and down the cliff side billowing in the breeze. The rush of cold air and the spray of cool mist hit her face.

The dinosaur let out a wail as it plummeted over the ledge behind her. River saw this out of the corner of her eye, and then noticed something else. Just in front of her, a long, narrow projectile came into view. River realized it was a thin, corroded rail of a long-collapsed railroad bridge. There wasn't much left of the structure: a few sticks of rotten railroad ties strung between a double set of rails. Almost nothing remained of the steel cables and support struts that once held the bridge safely in the air. It hadn't even been visible from the far bank.

Yet it was something, and River felt a rush of adrenaline as she realized the Boneshaker was about to come down on the track. She raised herself in the seat, bracing herself for the landing. She eased back on the throttle, leaning slightly as she tried to make the *boneshaker* line up with the rail.

River's guts twisted up as she closed in. She wasn't going to make it. The *boneshaker* had turned in the air. The tires weren't going to line up... In a desperate attempt to save her life, River dumped the bike. She pushed away from the handlebars, rising to stand with one foot on the edge of the seat and the other on the frame. The bike twisted beneath her, rolling out of control.

The landing was immediate and terrifying. The bike went down, landing sideways on the rusted rail beneath her. A spray of sparks went up and the sound of shrieking metal filled her ears. For a moment, she stood perfectly balanced on the bike as it went gliding down the track. It hit a rivet and jumped slightly. River steadied herself. A heartbeat later, the front tire struck an old piece of wood on the left side. It was all that remained of the bridge's original framework.

The bike jolted, swinging her around one hundred and eighty degrees. River suddenly found herself facing backwards. She twisted, glancing back and forth for an escape. The canopy of trees stretched out over the chasm, well out of reach. The opposing rail, several yards to her right, was also out of reach. Out of the corner of her eye, she saw something else that made her blood freeze: the rail she was riding was about to end.

River turned, bending her knees slightly, lowering her center of gravity. In her right hand, she uncoiled the whip she had brought. With a quick *snap!* the serpentine weapon shot out and latched onto a limb overhead. Simultaneously, the *boneshaker* slid out from underneath her. It shot over the end of the rail and went tumbling into the abyss.

River's momentum drove her forward, swinging away from the broken rail and towards the far side of the ravine. At the apex of her swing, River released her grip on the whip handle. She somersaulted through the air, landing at the very edge of the embankment with her legs hanging over the precipice. The soft earth gave way beneath her, rocks and soil tumbling down into the crevice.

River clawed at the ground, digging her nails into the damp soil. She couldn't find enough of a handhold to support her weight. Inch by inch, she went sliding back over the edge. Her fingers closed around a thick vine that had been invisible in the undergrowth. She grasped it tight with both hands as she went over the edge of the cliff.

The vine went tight, and River found herself dangling four hundred feet in the air. Below her, the *boneshaker* bounced off the cliff wall and hit the river with a barely audible *splash*. She winced as it sank beneath the frothing whitecaps. A spray of mist hit her in the face, bringing tears to her eyes, and the echoing roar of the waves filled her ears.

Chapter 4

Kale's battle with the knights went on for some time. It involved the use of numerous small and improvised weapons, including the previously mentioned dagger, as well as pieces of the broken card table, a steel gauntlet, and a sizeable length of lumber. Kale had no idea where the latter item originated, but he knew exactly what it felt like breaking across his back.

When all was said and done, there were three broken noses, one broken jaw, a handful of broken ribs, and a couple handfuls of missing teeth. Somehow, Kale managed to come out of the ordeal with only minor injuries, not the least of which was a cracked rib that gave him a sharp pain every time he took a deep breath. His knuckles were raw and bleeding, his left eye was swollen and discolored, and he had more cuts and bruises than he could count.

Despite all that, the commander managed to make it down to the gates with three men in tow. The young knight Flynn -who had started the fight- was there, along with Hector and Bathus. Flynn had a few bruises and a slight limp, but his only major injury was to his pride. Kale felt confident the youth wouldn't question his authority a second time. Hector hadn't been present for the fight (he had been at the forge at the time) and Bathus had only taken a few blows before deciding it wasn't worth the trouble. The middle-aged knight's bruises would heal soon enough.

Kale looked his crew over as they inspected their mounts for the journey. Sir Hector's mechanical charger was a deep midnight blue with a black mane and intricate engravings of his family crest and other decorative patterns on the armor. He wore a suit of polished silver plate, enhanced with spring-powered joints and bucklers with automatically extending spinning blades that were equally capable of breaking a sword blade or severing an opponent's limbs. The enhanced joints gave Hector greater strength and physical abilities than a normal man. Unfortunately, the extra weight of these enhancements would slow him down once the springs ran out. As far as Kale was concerned, such things were better suited to the arena than the real world, where they might fail without warning and lead to all sorts of calamities.

Sir Bathus was a full head taller than Hector, being nearly equal to Kale in size and stature, and wore armor painted a glossy black. His mount was black as well (like Kale's, but not as large), and when he sat astride the charger, it was almost impossible to tell where the knight ended and the horse began. He carried a kite shield that bore his family crest but no other decoration.

Gavin, who had been waiting for them at the gate, wore a mix of plate and leather armor similar to Kale's. This combination was specifically designed for lightness and articulation, and while being less protective than plate armor, it gave the knights the ability to move quickly during battle, and to fight longer with less fatigue. Gavin's charger was copper colored, and the gaps in the plate armor exposed large bronze gears and brass fittings inside.

The youngest of the group was Sir Flynn. Flynn was smaller than the other men, and his choices reflected that fact. He wore leather armor and fought primarily with a short, one-handed sword, wielding a dagger in his off hand. This was a light combination that was deadly and fast, but at the sacrifice of better protection offered by heavier armor and shields. Likewise, his deep green charger was smaller than the others, but more agile, faster, and more functional in close quarters such as a forest or in the thick of combat.

As Kale mounted up next to Gavin, the older knight looked him up and down with a wry grin. "How'd it go?" he said, staring at Kale's swollen eye.

"Great," Kale said with a sullen glare.

Sir Gavin couldn't contain his laughter. He threw his head back and roared until his eyes began to water. Kale didn't see the humor in the situation, and he said as much. Gavin replied:

"You got rocks for brains, boy. Didn't I tell you fighting them wouldn't get you anywhere?"

"We're here, aren't we?"

"Parts of you are," Gavin said, glancing over the four of them. "Ain't a single one of you in one piece, except for Hector. You should be in the infirmary, not on horseback."

"We'll be fine," Kale assured him. "Let's get moving."

Kale took the lead, guiding his charger down the road towards Stormwatch with the others following closely behind. They skirted the palace on their way through town and headed west, across the ancient lava flows. A cold wind blew down from the north, stirring up dust that stung their eyes and drove into their skin like tiny needles. Hector and Bathus lowered the faceplates on their helms, and Flynn produced a riding hat with built-in goggles. Kale put his head down and focused his attention on the path ahead.

Their charger's hooves made dull ringing sounds against the ground that the wind swept away before they had barely reached the riders' ears. The mounts' internal springs and gears were continuously *clicking* and making other small noises that Kale and the others had long since learned to ignore. Mostly, the knights heard the wind whistling through their armor and the occasional nerve-wracking screeches of a family of vultures that had taken interest in the group.

The trek across the barren lava fields took more than two hours. The group finally made it to the shelter of the forest just after noon. The trails here were narrow, winding up and down through the foothills, dropping into steep ravines and crossing fast-moving but shallow streams, forcing the group to ride single-file.

The wind continued to blow, shaking the treetops and periodically rattling loose dead limbs that came crashing to the ground around them. This, along with the eerie moaning sounds made by the trees in the wind, kept the men on edge. An unnatural silence seemed to pervade the woods, and it seemed to amplify every sound they made: the rattle of their armor was like breaking glass, the cracking branches under the charger's hooves were like gunshots. Silent as they tried to be, there was no escaping a certain amount of noise, not the least of which were the constant *clicking* noises of the mechanisms inside their spring-powered mounts, which although subtle and normally unnoticed, seemed now to take on a malevolence that gnawed at their nerves.

Not long after entering the woods, Kale felt the hairs stand up on the back of his neck. He paused a moment to look around. He glanced at Gavin. The elder knight was turning his head warily from side to side, his eyes scanning the dark woods around them. His right hand rested on his lap, never more than a few inches from the hilt of his sword.

"Somebody's watching us," Gavin said under his breath.

Kale nodded. They searched the woods for a few more seconds, but saw nothing. "Stay sharp," Kale said to the others, and then heeled his mount forward.

Eventually, when Flynn grew bored of the monotony, he made a few attempts at humor. His jests were met with dry sarcasm and dark glares that quickly silenced him. Kale was glad to see the young man recovering from their fight so rapidly. It reminded him of what it was like to be that age, when every injury seemed insignificant and every danger a challenge.

By way of comparison, every time his horse stumbled, Kale felt like he'd been kicked in the ribs, and the swelling around his left eye throbbed with every footfall. He continuously found himself daydreaming about a hot steaming bath back in Dragonwall, only to be snapped back to reality by a sudden jolt or a loud noise. His companions weren't faring much better. Only Gavin and Hector seemed reasonably alert. Kale attributed that less to the knights' age and experience and more to the fact that they hadn't been brawling with the others.

At one point, they came over a rise and saw distant smoke churning up into the sky. "We're too late," Gavin said with a dark frown.

"What are you talking about?" said Kale.

"That is Ravenwood."

The group picked up speed, but only briefly. Soon, the woods closed back in around them, and the awkward terrain made anything faster than a trot impossible. Not long after that, the scent of burning lumber and tar filled the air, and the smoke in the woods thickened into an acrid black fog. They pressed on, the sense of unease growing with every passing step.

The group reached Ravenwood just after sunset. The five knights sat motionless astride their mounts at the top of a hill, looking down at the burning ruins of the village. A handful of structures remained intact, though it was difficult to get a clear view through the black smoke churning up around them. It rose like a column into the sky, blocking out what little starlight there was before being swept away by the wind.

Kale sat astride his great black mechanical warhorse, one hand gripping the reins, the other unconsciously sliding toward the handle of the great sword bound to his saddle. Kale rarely used the weapon -it had come with the charger, and he preferred the two swords he always wore on his back- but he liked having it within easy reach. One could never have too many weapons at hand. Kale glanced at Sir Gavin a few feet off to his left, and at then the other knights.

"This can't be the place," he said. "The messenger said they had been attacked, but I didn't expect anything like this."

"This *is* Ravenood," Gavin said, his voice gravelly and low. "Or, it *was* Ravenwood."

Hector spoke up: "It would have taken a full day, more likely a day and a half to make the journey to

Stormwatch on foot. This must have happened right after the messenger left."

Kale pressed his heels to the kick-plates, driving his charger forward. They made a quick descent to the main road, and guided their mounts into town. The horses' steel hooves rang against the cobblestones, the sound accompanying the *crackling* of the fires around them. Smoke hung thick in the air, the scent of burning buildings mingling with that of burning flesh. Bodies lay strewn across the cobblestone streets, some dismembered, most had even been beheaded.

The branches overhead stirred as some creature scurried through the canopy. Kale snapped to attention, his hand unconsciously reaching for the handle of his sword as his eyes focused on a squirrel zooming along the limbs. He drew his gaze back to the street.

The smithy remained mostly intact, but only because it was made of stone. A few similar buildings in the area still stood, their scorched walls and burned roofs a silent testament to the horrors that had taken place only hours before. Kale stopped his charger and dismounted next to one of the decapitated bodies.

"Middle-aged man," he said in a quiet voice. "This is strange."

"Of course it is," said Flynn. "Somebody cut his head off!"

"Not that," said Kale. "Look, the neck wound is smooth, clean. There's no blood. The chest wound killed him. His shirt is soaked with blood..."

"You mean somebody cut his head off *after* he died?" said Bathus.

Kale's only response was a grim frown.

"Devils," Flynn said under his breath. "What happened here?"

"Look at his hands," Gavin said.

Kale twisted so that he could see the cadaver's hands. He narrowed his eyebrows, studying the bizarre injury, and then lifted the arm so the others could see.

"Something chewed his fingers off," said Sir Bathus. "One of those squirrels, maybe."

"I don't think so," Kale said. "Look closer. The fingers are worn smooth, right to the bone. There aren't any teeth marks."

"I'll be-" said Gavin, leaning forward in his saddle. "Couldn't have filed 'em any flatter than that."

"What are you saying?" said Flynn. "That he was clawing at the cobblestones with his fingers until they wore down to nothing?"

Kale stepped around the body and began examining the paving stones. "He was pulling himself. See these marks? This trail goes all the way across the village."

"Why would he do that?" said Hector.

Kale turned, studying the smoldering ruins and corpses surrounding them. "I have a better question. What happened to his head?"

They turned in their saddles, surveying the area. "Whoever killed him must have taken it," said Gavin. "I bet it's the same with the others."

"Why?" said Kale. "Why take a man's head?"

The other knights stared at him. No one had an answer. Kale climbed onto his charger.

"Split up and search for survivors. Call out if you find anything." He heeled his mount to a slow walk and rode around the smithy, where he found several more decapitated bodies. As Gavin had predicted, the heads were all missing. Kale rode around them and continued on, peering through the broken windows and charred remains of the burned buildings.

At the end of the street, he found a school -or, at least he assumed it was a school from the childlike drawings posted in the windows. In all likelihood, it performed as a town hall on Fridays and a temple on Sundays. From what he'd learned of Danaise, this was how things seemed to work in most of the kingdom. Resources were scarce, as was manpower, and most government buildings served multiple purposes.

The two-story brick building remained mostly intact. Kale saw a few broken windows, and some charring on one wall near the next building, but otherwise it seemed relatively unscathed. He dismounted and climbed the front steps, peering into the darkened windows.

Kale paused at the doors. He glanced up the street behind him, and his gaze lingered on one of the headless corpses. What if he found the same thing inside the school? What if the children had all been murdered? The thought sent bile churning up in his stomach.

Kale had seen the brutalities of war; had lived with them for the better part of his life. He'd seen the Vangar overlords beat and slaughter innocent men and women. He'd seen good people tortured and enslaved. Kale had sworn to kill every Vangar who ever crossed his path, and he'd done a pretty good job of it. If he had one goal in life, it was to make sure the Vangars could never do that again. But this was different. It was one thing to stare down at the corpse of a fallen enemy, another thing entirely to see the body of an innocent child.

No fear had ever stayed Kale's hand before -not even the bloodcurdling horror of facing down a thirty-foot dragon- but the thought of what might lie behind those doors froze him in his tracks. The warrior stood there a full minute battling this inner turmoil. At last, he took a deep breath, twisted the handle, and shoved the door open.

The room was dark, lit only by the soft glow of moonlight through the hazy windows. The scent of candle fat was strong in the air, the faint odor of hardwood and the lingering smoke of incense clinging to the curtains and the walls. The silence was oppressive, almost like a distant buzzing noise in his ears. He took a few steps, and the sound of his boot heels shattered the still.

Pews lined the floor. A doorway to his right opened into a small classroom filled with desks. An altar stood at the far end of the room with a tall cross looming behind. The serpentine form of a dragon stood on the beam of the cross, with its long tail spiraling down around the post. The creature's face leered down at him with a frightening realism. The golden eyes glistened in the darkness, the slavering tongue crimson red against ivory teeth. Kale felt a chill crawl down his spine.

"I see you," said a child's voice behind him.

Kale spun. He saw a young boy, perhaps seven or eight years old, halfway across the room. The child was dressed in proper clothes: a dark blue jacket with silver clasps and matching breeches, tall black boots and a bright white shirt with ruffles at the neck and sleeves. He stood in a shadowy spot between the pews, and seemed to shimmer with an unearthly aura of light.

"Who are you?" Kale said. "What happened here?"

"Have you seen my mommy?" said the child.

Kale took a step closer. The boy instantly vanished. The commander's blood froze. He approached the spot where the boy had been standing, and bent down, looking under the pews. He found nothing there but dust and shadows.

Before Kale could make any sense of the situation, he heard a shout. He raced back outside to stand on the front porch, eyes searching for the source.

"Over here!" Gavin shouted. Kale located the older knight a few hundred yards to the west, standing next to one of the burned-out shells. Kale leapt onto his mount and heeled the charger into a gallop. The creature's metal hooves threw up sparks against the pavestones as it sped down the street. An overturned wagon blocked his path, but Kale pulled on the reins and drove his heels into the accelerator panels. With a bit of deft maneuvering, he activated the five different controls at once required for a jump. The charger reared, clearing the wagon in a single leap.

The landing on the other side was a bit rough. The jolt nearly threw Kale out of the saddle, and he had to cling to the horn to right himself. Doing so caused a slight jerk on the reins, which made the charger veer to the left. The momentum threatened to throw him from the horse, but Kale held on. Somehow, he managed to tighten the reins. The speed came down to a healthy trot.

Kale guided the mount over to Gavin, and the elder knight watched him with a serious look as Kale dismounted. It wasn't like Gavin to miss an opportuneity to poke fun at Kale's riding skills. As he touched down, the charger snorted and blew a few rings of steam out through its nostrils. This was how the horse cooled its internal mechanisms to avoid overheating.

The steed had numerous such behaviors. While modeled after the movements and actions of real horses, they served the important purpose of maintaining the machine's complex inner workings. At times, their complexity reminded him of Socrates -although Socrates wasn't just a sophisticated piece of technology, but in fact a thinking, sentient being.

Sir Gavin led Kale around a burned-down cottage. There, on the ground by an old well, they saw the writhing body of a man with no arms. He was moaning and twisting helplessly, and a sense of compassion overwhelmed Kale. The warrior rushed in to help, but Gavin caught him by the shoulder.

"Stay back!" he warned. "That thing isn't human."

The noise of Gavin's voice attracted the creature's attention. It twisted, turning its head so it could see them. The creature's eyes were dead, a glazed-over powdered blue color. Most of the flesh was gone from its skull, revealing a grinning skeletal face and a hollow opening where its nose should have been.

"Devils," said a voice behind them. Kale glanced over his shoulder and realized the other knights had arrived. Young Sir Flynn looked as pale as a sheet.

"I know what this is," Kale said. "These people have been exposed to starfall. After they die, it activates something in their brains so that they seem alive, but they're not."

"It looks alive to me," said Sir Hector.

"Not alive or dead," Kale said. "Somewhere between: *un-dead.*"

"I've heard stories of this," said Gavin. "But I've never seen it before."

"I don't understand," said Hector. "We've lived with starfall all our lives, but I've never seen this happen in Dragonwall."

"You haven't been exposed to it," said Kale. "Not like him. You locked yourselves inside when the dragon's breath came. You capped your wells, and covered your gardens. These people... I guess they didn't know."

"They knew," said Gavin. "This is why the people of the outer villages always burn the bodies of the dead."

"They knew this would happen?"

Gavin tilted his head. "There are stories... legends. I think most people don't really believe them anymore, but they continue to burn the bodies of their dead for religious purposes. They believe a corpse must be burned at sunset, in order to expedite the journey into the afterlife."

"The practice began as a way to prevent this from happening?" Kale said. "And it became a religion?"

Gavin shrugged. "Religion and tradition are intertwined for these people. Men do many things they don't truly understand; things that are passed down to them from their forefathers. Children are taught to do things a certain way. They grow up and teach those things to their children, and so on for generations. Eventually, something that was once done out of common sense becomes an unquestionable creed, even if the practice has outlived its usefulness."

"Or, in this case, the reason is forgotten, but the practice is still necessary."

"Exactly."

"So what happened to him?" Hector said, nodding at the undead creature slavering on the ground before them. "Why didn't they burn him?"

"I think I understand," said Kale. "When the raiders attacked the village, they left the dead lying in the streets. There will be more like him nearby."

"I doubt it," said Gavin.

Kale frowned. "What do you mean?"

"The heads, remember? Someone took their heads. Whoever did it must've missed this one."

Kale drew one of his swords. He decapitated the creature in one swift stroke. The movement instantly ceased. He sheathed his sword and stepped around the others, heading back to his horse.

"Where are you going?" said Gavin.

"To find a safe place for a fire. There's nothing else we can do tonight. Tomorrow, we'll find out what happened here and report back to the queen."

Chapter 5

In Kale's absence, Shayla found Dragonwall ominously quiet. Leaning over the balcony rail, she saw a handful of men working down in the forge, their lean muscular forms glistening in the orange glow of the volcanic lava. They swung their hammers in smooth, controlled motions, and the anvils rang like so many bells, but the sound was stifled, compressed, like a pillow-covered scream.

The skies had darkened shortly after the commander's departure, and now a drizzle had begun falling into the cone of the mountain. The rain evaporated into steam long before it reached the bottom. The humidity coalesced into a vaporous fog that drifted cloud-like through the center of the mountain, spilling out across the balconies and walkways, intensifying the already palpable gloom.

She turned, walking along the long, sweeping road that curved around the inside of the mountain. Perhaps it was the fog, Shayla thought, that had driven everyone into their private chambers for the evening. Or perhaps it was the somber mood that had permeated the place since the death of King Dane, or the death of yet another fine laborer; the man whose body had been found that very morning, dosed by a poison no doubt administered by someone who once had loved him but could no longer tolerate his unrestrained cruelty.

Barbarians, Shayla thought with a grimace. *Every single one of them...*

So what if she had taught the women the use of poisons? That didn't mean the blood was on her hands, did it? After all, these men didn't have to continue forcing themselves on these poor women, beating them, mistreating them in a thousand different ways... Somehow, they had to learn.

Eventually, they would have to stop making excuses and start taking responsibility for their behavior. They would have to start behaving like civilized human beings, rather than animals incapable of controlling their own behavior.

Unlikely, she thought with a sigh. If there was one thing Shayla had learned from the men of Dragonwall, it was that they had an unlimited capacity to excuse their own sins. It wasn't unique to this place, of course. Narcissism was a remarkably persistent human condition, and Shayla had found that nearly everyone was capable of this type of self-validation. She was no exception. She had made mistakes, betrayed trusts. Now, she had even taken action that had led to numerous deaths.

But it was one sort of crime to kill a man, and something else entirely to *murder* a man. Yes, there was a difference, and it played a crucial role in determining the difference between a hero and a criminal, between a soldier and a psychopath. Shayla considered herself the former, and her victims the latter. Even that was taking too much credit. After all, it wasn't Shayla killing these men, it was their own wives. That in itself had to say something about the relative morality of the situation.

"Hey, girlie."

Shayla froze mid-step. The raspy voice had come out of the shadows to her right. She focused her attention there, her right hand instinctively retrieving the bladed fan from her sleeve. A face appeared. It was a long face, pale, almost skeletal, with deep sunken eyes that glared at her, and close-cropped hair that fell in a straight line across the broad forehead.

"What do you want?" she said, taking a step back.

The man who emerged from the tunnel wasn't familiar to her, but he shared the look of many of the others inside Dragonwall. Short, broad, pale... too pale. Unhealthy in the way that a man can become when he spends too much time in the dark, and begins to forget where to draw the line between the shadows of the mountain and the darkness in the recesses of his own mind.

"I've been meanin' to talk to you, girlie," he said. His voice was sharp, strangely high. A sure sign of an unhinged mind. Shayla brought the fan up, but before she could open it to expose the blades, someone grabbed her from behind.

Shayla struggled, tried to pull away, but the attacker held her in a vice-like grip. He squeezed her wrists until she cried out, and the fan slid from her fingers.

One by one, seven more men appeared out of the shadows. Some emerged from the tunnel. Some came walking up the balcony from below, or from behind her. She didn't know who they were, but one thing was clear: they had planned this. They had been lying in wait for her.

"Hurry," said the man with the skeleton face. "Bring her this way!"

They pushed a bag over her head, and Shayla felt herself lifted from the ground. They carried her down the slope a ways, and then turned into one of the many tunnels branching off to the sides. They wormed their way through the mountain for a few minutes, leaving Shayla no sense whatsoever of where they had gone.

At last, they descended a short flight of stairs and entered some sort of small stone chamber. She could tell that much from the sound of their boots and their low voices echoing around her. She could also hear water: a slow *drip, drip, drip* somewhere nearby.

They pulled off the hood. Shayla blinked. It was dark, the entire room lit only by one torch in the hands of one of her captors. The room, it seemed, was not so much a chamber as a subterranean cavern. The ceiling was ten feet high, and the room was approximately twenty feet in diameter. At the center stood a fountain carved out of stone. The steady drip she had heard was a milky substance running out of the limestone overhead to land in the center of the pond. The water there was milky, too, and it cast a pale green luminescence about the room.

"Starfall," she said in a whisper.

"That's right," said the man.

"What are you doing? Why did you bring me here?"

"We know what's been going on," he said. "Did you think we wouldn't find out?"

"Find out what? You're insane!"

There was a shuffling noise across the room, and Shayla realized that a woman had joined them. She was young, no more than seventeen, dressed in the simple garments of a laborer. But she was pretty. Too pretty for her own good. Shayla's eyebrows narrowed. She recognized the widow of the latest murder victim.

"Dinah?"

Jamie Sedgwick

Dinah threw her gaze to the floor. "I'm sorry. I didn't mean to tell... They were going to *hurt me.*"

Shayla pressed her lips together, fighting back the curses. *It's not her fault. She's just a frightened child...*

"That's right," said the man. "She told us everything. We know who they got the poisons from. We know what you've been up to."

"Then you know every one of you is going to die."

He struck her with the back of his hand, and Shayla cried out as stars filled her vision. A hot, throbbing pain swelled across her cheek. She could feel her lips going numb. She shook the pain off, blinking to clear her vision.

"When Kale gets back-"

"He's got a surprise comin', too."

They locked eyes, and he grinned from ear to ear. "Put her over there, boys. Time to teach her a lesson."

They dragged Shayla to the center of the room. She fought them every step of the way. They exclaimed at her strength, but against all of them Shayla was helpless. They forced her onto her back, bent uncomfortably over the rim of the fountain, facing the ceiling. Shayla's hair dangled down into the starfall, and the milky water dripped from the ceiling onto her face. The skeleton man appeared in front of her.

"Now it's our turn to poison you," he said. He put his hand over her face and forced Shayla's head down into the water. She fought with every ounce of strength she had. She jerked her arms, kicked her legs, twisted her hands, trying to break free. One of the men lost his grip on her and in a flash, Shayla had a stiletto in her hand. She swung it wildly, unable to see her target. She felt the tip penetrate soft flesh. Her victim ran screaming from the room.

They caught her wrist, squeezing it painfully until Shayla dropped the knife. Instantly, they shoved her head back into the water. The starfall felt strange against her skin, slightly warm, and it burned the soft tissue in her nose and her eyes. Just when it seemed she had run out of air and couldn't fight it any longer, her head came up out of the water. Shayla gasped.

The moment she opened her mouth, someone began to pour water over her face. Shayla coughed, gagging as she struggled to keep the water out of her lungs. It coursed through her sinuses, burning like acid. Her eyes ached from the pressure. Her heart drummed in her chest. When she could fight no more, Shayla's body took over, and she sucked in a breath. The oxygen gurgled through the moisture trapped in her throat. Her lungs filled with air, but it hurt in a way that she had never imagined.

She coughed and sputtered, her limbs convulsing, eyes rolling back in her head. Before she could draw another breath, they shoved her back under. At some level, Shayla knew she wasn't drowning -not yet, anyway- but her body refused to believe.

This went on for some time, until Shayla began to lose consciousness. At last, her body went limp and she lost all strength to resist. The sound of their wicked laughter rang in her ears. A numb warmth spread through her limbs. Her captors released her, and Shayla fell to the floor, coughing, whimpering, her body shivering violently.

The men were silhouettes in the flickering torchlight. They faded into the tunnel, the echoes of their shuffling feet diminishing in the distance. The blue-green glow of the starfall barely illuminated the chamber. The ceiling went in and out of focus. The sound of her heartbeat filled Shayla's ears.

She rolled onto her side and her arm fell across a piece of fur. One of the men had lost his cloak. Shayla pulled it over herself, a low whimper escaping her lips. The room spun, and she lost consciousness.

Chapter 6

River wasn't sure how long she had been dangling over the edge of the cliff. It could have been minutes, or just a few frantic seconds. With her adrenaline up and her heart thudding like a steamhammer, time lost all meaning. A familiar fear was churning up inside her, working its way into her consciousness.

River had been forced to confront her acrophobia on multiple occasions, and each time she gained a bit more control. But it was never easy, and at moments like this, it was almost too much to face. It was all she could do to fight down the rising panic in her chest. She closed her eyes, tried not to think about the four hundred foot drop below.

In her mind's eye, River saw the whitewater rapids crashing against sharp rocks, the spray of water over the swirling eddies waiting to swallow her whole. The sound of the river filled her ears, echoing up and down the ravine, a deep endless rumble that she could feel as much as hear.

She took a deep breath and opened her eyes. A misty breeze whipped up in her face, sprinkling her skin and eyelashes with tiny droplets of moisture. In her hand, the inch-thick vine was wet and slick. Her grip was tenuous at best, and she knew all too well how dangerous it would be to let go for even a second. Then again, she *had to* let go, if she wanted to climb out of there. One hand would have to move. Then the other...

Ultimately, it wasn't self-discipline or willpower that won the battle for her. It was the sudden jerk of the vine as something gave way up above. River dropped a few inches, and came to a sudden stop. The vine slipped in her grip, and she slid a bit farther before tightening her grip. The pit of her stomach dropped all the way to the bottom.

In a rising panic, River slid her hand up and closed it around the vine. It was a quick, erratic movement; the result of sheer terror more than anything else, but it was a success. River strained her muscles, pulling herself up a few inches. She summoned her courage and repeated the movement. This time, she reached farther, hoping to close the gap.

In short time, River found herself approaching the embankment at the top of the cliff. It jutted outward in a way that seemed impossible to surmount, but she eventually found a foothold in the rocks. She gave herself a little push, swinging her legs outward over the ravine, and then pulled herself over the outcropping.

She grunted, digging up handfuls of soft earth as she clambered over the ledge. Her legs kicked, swinging left and right, feet searching for a foothold. Then, suddenly, she was up and over and back on solid ground. River rolled onto her back, panting, staring at a crack of blue sky peeking through the canopy of green. The scent of rich earth and jungle filled her nostrils, and the forest seemed to come to life around her. Brightly colored birds flitted back and forth among the trees. Tiny simian creatures rested on the branches overhead, shrieking, glaring at her. Somewhere across the river, something large thudded through the underbrush.

River pushed to her feet as she took in her surroundings. The abandoned railroad tracks led up the hill and into the jungle behind her. The whip that had saved her life still hung from the overhead branch, some twenty feet away. Next to her, at the bottom of the ravine...

River couldn't help herself. She walked up to the ledge and leaned over, scanning the rapids below for a sign of her beloved *boneshaker*. She didn't see so much as a fender or a glimmer of brass in the river below.

The loss of the machine left an ache in her heart. It was like losing Tinker all over again. Tinker had conceived the original steamcycle when she was just a child. She had helped him work on it over the years, and eventually engineered a few improvements, like the cushioned seat and the coil-spring shocks.

On the day Tinker died, River had escaped from the Vangars on his *boneshaker*. That machine had been destroyed, but River's new *boneshaker* had been modeled on the original, with a few minor improvements. Superficially, it was almost exactly like Tinker's. And now it was gone.

River scanned the cliffs in either direction, looking for another crossing point. She didn't see anything promising, so she started into the jungle, following the old tracks. She moved at a brisk pace, her senses on high alert as she brushed aside the ferns and branches that blocked her path. Overhead, a group of monkeys followed along, occasionally letting out wild screeches to warn her that she was in their territory. River didn't pay much attention. She wasn't worried about tiny monkeys or other small jungle creatures. It was the massive dragon-kin Socrates called dinosaurs that had her concerned.

Once or twice, River strayed from the path and found herself in dense, impassable jungle. It quickly became apparent that she could not progress any farther without a machete -or, preferably, a steamscout equipped with a saw blade- and so she returned to the tracks. Eventually, the land sloped upwards and River made a short climb to the top of a hill. As she came over the rise, she got a bird's-eye view of the surrounding jungle.

River caught her breath as her gaze fell on a massive stone pyramid in the distance. It was a few miles off, but it was so huge that it seemed like she could reach out and touch it. The structure had terraced steps or walkways leading up its face. Gardens lined the terraces, and while it was hard to tell from that distance, River was sure she saw people on the steps tending the plants and going in and out of the great entrance.

A tower of gears rose up alongside the pyramid, but from that distance, River couldn't be sure what purpose the mechanism served. At the very peak of the pyramid rose a shaft of some sort, like a lightning rod pointing up into the heavens.

Surrounding the great pyramid, River saw the caps of other, much smaller pyramids. She saw other signs of civilization as well: broad, clear-cut swaths through the jungle -these were almost certainly roads- and she caught glimpses of additional stone structures peeking out through the foliage. This, River realized, was a new civilization!

She turned in a slow circle, getting her bearings. It only took a second to realize that less than a mile back, she had completely bypassed a bridge over the river. This was an almost direct route back the way she had come. She made a mental map of the area, noting the large trees, boulders, and other landmarks that would help her find her way. Once she had picked out a path, River broke into a run.

A smile came to her lips. Socrates would be thrilled to hear of her discovery...

Chapter 7

Socrates and his crew rushed the wrecked train as soon as River was out of sight on her *boneshaker*. They were armed with muskets and swords, and ready for just about anything. They had seen movement inside the first passenger car, so Socrates led his team there first.

"Weapons ready!" he commanded, putting his hand on the door handle. They raised their bows and firearms. Socrates twisted the handle, and then he slid the door open.

There was a hissing sound, followed by a blood-curdling shriek. A dark shape came hurtling through the open door. The creature hit Socrates at full speed, with a surprising amount of force. The automaton stumbled back, dropping his musket as the mass of fur and flailing limbs bore him down. He fell off the stairs and landed on the slope next to the train.

The crew came forward with their weapons ready, but they couldn't fire without risking harm to the automaton. Socrates struggled alone against his assailant. Claws dug into his face and scalp. Fangs latched onto his forehead, gnawing, slavering. He fought valiantly, but could not seem to get the upper hand on this violent creature.

A minute passed, and finally after a heroic battle, the ape managed to get a grip on the beast with his left hand. He pulled it away from his face and held the creature at arm's length, studying it as it thrashed and screamed at him. It was surprisingly small, considering the battle it had put up. The creature bared its fangs, shrieking at him with a high-pitched rattle.

"What is that thing?" Micah said from the roof of the Iron Horse.

"A primate of some sort," said Socrates, tilting it back and forth. The little beast raged, clawing at his midnight blue fur, snarling and hissing at him.

"What's it saying?" That was Morgane, the young woman from Stormshield who had joined the crew after murdering her father. This latter part was a secret known only to Socrates. He swiveled his head to look at her.

"How should I know if it's saying anything at all?"

Thane, the tall, blond-haired bard doubled over with laughter. "You don't speak its language?" he said "It's obviously a relative of yours!"

Socrates glared at him. Morgane looked away in embarrassment.

Socrates snorted at the bard's idea of a joke and puff of steam rolled up from the exhaust pipe behind his ear. He lifted the creature up to the ledge of the roof, and it leapt from his hands. It scurried across the top of the railcar and climbed up into the nearby branches. He glanced at the rest of the crew, and they hurried to cover their grins.

"You've had your fun," he said. "Let's keep moving."

Socrates retrieved his musket and motioned for the others to follow as he stepped inside the train. Inside the passenger car, they found the bodies of three passengers. They were little more than skeletons. Thane poked one with the barrel of his blunderbuss, and it collapsed. The bones shattered as they fell to the floor, and the clothing turned to dust.

"Don't touch anything!" Socrates said angrily. "We don't know yet what killed these people. They may have been carrying a disease!"

Thane took a step back, eyeing the body uncertainly. Kynan, one of several Tal'mar warriors among the crew, lowered his bow and knelt down next to the remains.

"How long have they been here?" he said.

Socrates shook his head. "It's impossible to say. Possibly even centuries. They're wearing civilian clothing, so they must have been passengers. I suppose we will find the crew in one of the other cars."

He turned his head as he spoke, examining the roof of the compartment. He noted several broken pipes and a section of copper wiring hanging down. He examined them quickly, and then moved on to the next car without further statement.

The door was sealed, and it took some time to pry it open. When it finally released, there was a *hiss* of air rushing into the compartment. The scent of ancient death mingled with the sickly-sweet aroma of flowery perfume washed over them. Thane almost gagged. He hid his face in his elbow. Behind him, Morgane dropped the double-barreled scattergun she'd been carrying and covered her face with a kerchief. Socrates stepped inside, motioning for the others to follow.

This was another passenger car, almost identical to the first, and it contained more than a dozen occupants. Strangely, the bodies were so well preserved that they almost seemed alive. It was as if they had fallen asleep, and at that very moment been frozen in time. Their flesh was dry and leathery, as if the moisture had been sucked out, and although the bodies remained intact, the eyeballs were missing.

"What happened to them?" Thane said, leaning down to peer into the black eye sockets of a middle-aged man. The deceased passenger was wearing a long black coat and top hat that were perfectly preserved, and had a cane resting across his lap. If not for the awkward way he was slumped over in the seat, he almost seemed alive.

"This car was sealed at the time of the crash," Socrates said. "I believe there may have been a malfunction with the oxygen system. The air in this room was sucked out, causing these poor people to suffocate. The lack of oxygen most likely made them lose consciousness rather quickly."

A chill ran down the bard's spine. It was one thing to share a room with a few ancient skeletons. A railcar full of mummified corpses was entirely different. These remains still had *skin*. It was almost possible to imagine what they had looked like in life... in fact, they seemed not so far removed from it. For all appearances, they could have died just a few days ago.

"Next car?" Thane said, stifling a shiver.

Socrates grinned. "Perhaps you'd be more comfortable waiting outside with my *relatives*."

Thane didn't laugh. Apparently, the joke had run its course.

As they moved deeper into the train, they found twenty-three more skeletons. Some had died due to minor injuries, others to starvation. It was impossible to tell if any of the survivors had left the train. Morgane made a comment about this as they moved through the corridors towards the last few cars.

"If anyone escaped the accident, they may have gone for help," said Socrates, "but I doubt they made it far. I want to find the passenger manifest and the

Engineer's log. That's our only hope of understanding what caused all of this."

They heard a commotion outside, and Socrates leaned across one of the bench seats to gaze out the window. "River is back," he said, struggling to get the window open. It took a moment, but finally came free with a *pop!* He stuck his head out, and called to get her attention.

"Socrates!" River said, looking down the embankment from the tracks. "You won't believe what I found."

"Wait for me there," he said. "I'll be done here shortly."

They quickly explored the last few cars, but didn't find much of note. The cars were tilted at awkward angles, almost lying on their sides, which made the job particularly trying. Not long after that, they climbed out the rear of the train and hiked up to the Iron Horse to meet with River.

The mechanic told the others the story of her adventure, becoming increasingly excited as she talked. By the time she reached the end of her tale, River's words had strung into one long run-on sentence:

"...And there were gardens on the pyramids, but I couldn't see what they were growing, but there were people there -People, Socrates!- and they were working in the gardens, and the machine -I'm still not sure what it was, but it reminded me of the chronoforge, so maybe it's an energy source or something- and there was a lightning rod... Socrates, we need to hurry!"

Socrates watched her childish excitement with an amused grin. River's eyes were wide and sparkling, her shoulders thrown back, her hand gestures spirited and sweeping. When she finally stopped talking, she realized that he had been staring at her with a strange look on his face.

"What? What is it?" she said.

"I haven't seen you this excited in weeks. Not even when we found Dragonwall."

"Yes, well, the hallucinations sort of put a damper on my excitement then. Can we go now? Socrates you *have to* see this place. It's amazing!"

"Shortly. As soon as we locate the Engineer's log and the crew's manifest. In the meanwhile, why don't you search the train for anything useful?"

River's expression sank.

"It won't take long," Socrates promised.

River's lack of enthusiasm for the task was obvious. Nevertheless, she threw herself into her work. It wasn't hard to locate the cargo and engineering cars, but there was a bit of a struggle when it came to retrieving their inventories. These were the cars tilted at a difficult angle, and the cargo box was lying completely on its side.

At one point, Micah was helping her retrieve some tools and parts from the engineering car when he pulled a tarp away from the corner and discovered something of importance. "River!" he said, waving her over. "What is it?"

She held her lantern in the air and looked the object up and down. There was an armature with a spindle on the top, so River gave it a spin. It turned easily, idling along without any assistance or any sign of stopping. The bearings made light clicking sounds as the armature spun inside the copper windings.

"It's a motor," she said at last. "A large electric motor. I've never seen one so big... it must have been a prototype."

"Can we use it?" Micah said, his eyes wide in the darkness.

She looked down at him. The halfling's imp-like features were accentuated by the angle of the light, and he looked grotesque, almost like a gargoyle. Strangely, she found his appearance comforting. After all, Micah was without a doubt the nicest man she had ever met. At first, his appearance had seemed unusual to her, but now that she knew him well, the sight of Micah instantly brought a smile to her face.

"It's worthless," she said at last. "This technology is inferior to steam power. Just look how bulky this thing is. It must weigh a thousand pounds. And there's no way to power it. We would have to build a massive generator just to drive this thing, and for what? It can't do anything a steam engine couldn't do."

"Fair enough. Let's get out of here, then."

He started to leave, but River didn't move. She tapped her chin with her forefinger. "Then again, if I were to remove the armature and install a series of powerful magnets, I could convert it into a generator..."

"Can we use one of those?" Micah said.

River frowned. "I don't know. Let's take it, just in case. We'll need the crane."

Micah sighed.

The decision added three hours to their salvage operation. Half that time was spent assembling and disassembling the crane. Once the operation was underway, they had a huge struggle to get the motor out of the corner and across the overturned railcar. Unfortunately, this was the only way to get the motor close to the railcar's door where it was accessible to the crane. It was back-breaking work, and required almost the entire crew, some pulling ropes, others pushing inside the car. When it was all said and done, the actual lifting part done by the crane took all of ten minutes. By then it was dark, and Vann had already rung the dinner bell.

"I hope it was worth the trouble," River said to Socrates as she checked the tie-downs connecting the motor to the floor of one of the cargo cars.

"It's a good find," he said. "I'm sure we'll put it to good use."

"What about the city?" River said. "Can we go now?"

Socrates frowned. "Not just yet. There are too many variables when approaching a new civilization. After all, remember what happened when we pulled into Dragonwall?"

"I suppose," she said with a sigh. "Tomorrow, then?"

"Yes, tomorrow. First thing."

River couldn't conceal her disappointment. She left, stepping out into the passageway and ambling up the train towards the dining car. She understood her commander's logic, but that didn't do anything to stem her excitement over the discovery. For River, the best part of their journey was finding new and exciting things; things that no one had ever seen before. The civilization she had glimpsed earlier that day was the very definition of that. And the pyramids! What were they for? Who had built them? Her mind reeled at the possibilities.

The entire crew had gathered in the dining car, and after a hard day's work, they were all feeling rambunctious. The conversation was loud and boisterous, and already several people had started drinking and playing darts. As soon as dinner was over, they would clear the tables and the serious relaxation would start.

River didn't care to stick around for any of that. She filled a plate and took it back to her quarters. Pirate, the raccoon that had become the crew's mascot, followed her through the passages. They passed through several cars before he finally succeed in getting her attention. First, he rubbed up against her leg and made a purring sound. When River ignored that, he barked at her. Finally, he scurried ahead of her and stopped in the middle of her path, standing upright on his hind legs. He held out one palm before her like a beggar.

"Forget it," River said. "You're already too fat."

Pirate made a sniffling sound and jammed his tiny fists into his eyes as if he were crying. River rolled her eyes. "Fine," she said, tossing him a bit of buttery bread crust. "Just don't expect me to cry for you when you drop dead of a heart attack."

Pirate didn't hear her comment because he was already halfway back to the dining car.

River ate her dinner and spent an hour studying before going to bed. She had several books in her bunkroom about reading and writing. Micah had already helped her understand some of the basics, the way certain shapes represented phonetic sounds, and the way those letters might be combined into a word. It was a surprisingly simple concept, and she wondered why she'd never grasped it before. Perhaps it hadn't been important. Frankly, the only reason it was important now was because she wanted to be able to read some of the engineering manuals stored in the train's library. River seemed to have reached the limits of her understanding, and without an outside source of knowledge, she simply couldn't learn any more.

Socrates was there, of course, and he had some advanced knowledge on the topics of engineering and mechanics. Unfortunately, the ape was usually too busy managing the train and the crew to sit with her for any period of time. And when it came down to it, River was better off having access to that information when she wanted and needed it, rather than waiting for Socrates to have the time for her.

She composed a few sentences, checked them for errors, and then set her books aside. It had been a long, exhausting day. Especially the latter part. Stringing letters into words was more trying than repairing a boiler or even building a motor. She'd rather do just about anything else with her time... But there was only one way to learn, and she was determined.

River woke before the sun the next morning and was ready to go in minutes. After a quick, ice-cold rinse in her bunkroom's shower stall, River slipped into her canvas breeches and tall boots. She wore a white linen blouse under a burgundy-colored leather bodice, and a matching red bandana on her head to keep the sweat out of her eyes.

River's clothes had all been recently washed and were relatively new, which meant she was fairly well dressed, relatively speaking. Other women River had known -women like Shayla and Morgane- wouldn't be caught dead wearing breeches in public, much less an article of clothing made from leather. This was considered manly garb, and River's manner of dress was often viewed as "low," if not outright indecent by those people who considered themselves civilized.

River didn't care much about that. According to Tinker, she had inherited her loathing for skirts and dresses from her mother. The difference between the two of them was that Breeze had somehow managed to force herself to conform to social acceptance, wearing traditionally feminine clothing in order to satisfy societal expectations, whereas River wouldn't even entertain the idea. If society wanted her to dress a certain way, then society could go jump off a cliff. Preferably, the one she'd almost fallen off yesterday. While they were down there, maybe they could find the *boneshaker*.

That being said, River did make some effort to clean up her appearance, in order to make a good impression. There was no telling what the people of this marvelous new city would be like, and it did make sense to at least present a semi-respectful countenance. But she also went ahead and strapped on her gun, just in case. Things had gone wrong before...

River found Socrates at the locomotive. The fire had burned low overnight, and he was bringing it back up to temperature. After entering the crater, the commander had switched from starfall to lumber as the train's primary fuel. It was just a precaution, he had said. They now had an adequate supply of the starfall, but trees were a far more common and less valuable resource inside the crater. Better to save what fuel they had in case they needed it later. In the meanwhile, they pulled out their maps of the area, and River helped him to chart the city's location.

"If my memory is correct," she said, making a red mark on the chart, "this is the location of the bridge I crossed."

"It's located next to the tracks?" Socrates said. "I wonder why the steamscouts didn't note this in their sensor logs."

"They may not have seen it. The jungle is dense along the tracks, and the bridge is hardly visible until you're right on top of it."

"Was it steel?" Socrates said. His fingers made quiet *click-clicking* sounds as he scratched the fur on his chin. River narrowed her eyebrows.

"The bridge? No, it was stone. Why do you ask?"

"I'm trying to date this civilization. The engineer's logs from the other train didn't mention this city. I suppose I'll have to wait until we can get a closer look."

Socrates roused the crew with an announcement through the communication pipes. A short while later, they were on their way. It was only a few miles down the tracks to the bridge, but it still took nearly an hour to get there, and then to get the steamwagons unloaded from the train. The entire time, River was chomping at the bit. Her *boneshaker* had only been gone one day, and already she was missing it.

At last, they loaded up a group of armed fighters into two steamwagons. Socrates, River, Micah and Thane took the first wagon, while Vann and two of the Tal'mar -Loren and Kynan- took the second. As always, the Tal'mar were armed with bows, while the others took swords or blunderbusses.

The trip across the bridge and down the narrow jungle road took less than fifteen minutes. A quarter mile away from the pyramids, they began seeing signs of civilization. The trees in the area had been clear-cut to make way for buildings and farmland, and they began to see small farms and gardens along the roadway. The dwellings in this area were primarily huts and tents, but as they drew closer to the city, these gave way to buildings of stone, and finally, the pyramids themselves.

"They have no wall," Thane observed as they drew close. "How do they protect themselves from the jungle creatures, or enemies?"

No one had an answer. They passed some farmers working in the fields, and a handful of pedestrians walking along the roadway, but no one paid them any attention. Socrates was concerned about their dismissive behavior, and his frown deepened the closer they got to the city.

The people here were mostly dark skinned, though River noted a great deal of variation in the amount of pigment in their skin. None were as fair as Thane and River, but many had the golden hue of a deep tan, and others were darker, like Kale's old flame Rowena. Some were so black that they looked to River as if their skin had been dyed to match the darkest fabric.

For the most part, they dressed in robes of light, billowing cloth. The colorations varied from white and tan to deep hues of blue and purple. They seemed to prefer some contrasting color in their garb, usually in the form of stripes or other simple patterns. One item everyone wore, down to the youngest child, was sandals. This, she presumed, was to protect their feet from the plants and crawling things of the jungle.

Inside the city, the dirt roads became straight cobbled streets and pathways that met at perfect ninety-degree intersections. Lawns grew between the buildings and stretched out in long, perfectly manicured fields around the pyramids. A series of canals and aqueducts brought water from the jungle into town and dispersed it among the fields for irrigation. Alongside the tallest pyramid, River observed the massive truss-like clockwork structure that she had seen previously. It was several stories high and filled with slowly spinning cogs and gears. One of the larger canals fed into this machine and then vanished beneath the adjacent structure.

"What does it do?" River said under her breath.

While River was wondering at the engineering marvels, Socrates was trying to get the attention of the civilians. As the steamwagons slowed, the people continued walking by, paying no attention to them at all.

"Excuse me," Socrates said to a man they were passing. "Sir?"

The man averted his gaze. He turned aside and went scurrying back between the buildings. Socrates turned his attention to a woman carrying a basket of fruits and vegetables. "Good morning," he said. "Do you understand me?"

Likewise, she fixed her gaze on the ground and hurried off in another direction. Socrates exchanged a frustrated glance with River. He parked the steamwagon and approached several more people, but likewise, none would respond, much less look at him. Finally, the automaton lost his temper.

"Does anyone here know how to talk?" he shouted in a booming voice. "Anyone?"

"I speak your language, beast."

They all swung their heads around to see a man standing a few yards off, approximately half the distance between them and the smallest pyramid. He *appeared* to be a man, at least. He had the body of a man, but he wore a metal helm of some sort that glinted gold in the sunlight. He also wore a deep blue robe with gold stripes and hems, and gloves of pure white cloth. In his right hand, he carried a scepter-like metal rod made of gold.

"My name is Anu-Abas. I am the overseer of this colony."

A dark cloud seemed to pass over River as he made this statement. The last time she'd encountered someone called an overseer, it hadn't ended well. Her hand unconsciously slid toward the handle of her revolver. Socrates spoke:

"I'm Socrates, the commander of the Iron Horse. These are my companions. We've come here to study new cultures and civilizations, such as your own."

"That is unfortunate," said Anu-Abas, "for our culture has neither desire nor need of such examination." He came closer, and as he moved through the shadows of the trees and came into the light, River caught her breath. What she had perceived to be a helm was actually a bronze plate riveted to the side of his skull, and a brass framework with multi-colored glass lenses secured over his left eye.

The overseer's skin was drawn tight across his skull, like the mummified bodies they'd seen in the derailed train. His flesh was discolored, with patches of green and black decay, chunks of flesh missing entirely, revealing chalk-white bone underneath. His lips were thin, parted in a death-like grimace that revealed rotting yellow teeth.

The overseer's left leg was similarly braced with a framework of brass and bronze between the upper thigh and shin. The creature's knee was missing, and this mechanism apparently functioned as a replacement.

Anu-Abas, River realized with a sense of dread, was not human. He was *undead*.

The creature raised his scepter and pointed it at them. "You are not welcome here. I will not give you a second warning."

Chapter 8

The next morning, Kale found himself wandering alone among the ruins of Ravenwood. While he saw no sign of the missing heads, there were many heartbreaking mementos of the tragedy that had occurred in that place. The scorched and broken ruins of family heirlooms, children's toys, and pieces of art lay scattered all around him. There were bodies, too, mostly buried in ash. Kale left them and moved on.

He was searching through the debris when Gavin rode up on his copper steed. The older knight watched him from the saddle for a few seconds before speaking. "You all right, son?"

Kale glanced up at him. "Why do you ask?"

"You seem... uneasy. That's understandable, of course. This place has us all on edge. Burned buildings, decapitated bodies... It's one thing to attack an army or even a fortress, but what sort of monsters would do this to simple peasants?"

Kale bent over and lifted the charred remains of a toy. It had been a wooden farm animal -possibly a horse or a mule- at one time. Now, it was little more than charcoal.

"Gavin," Kale said, glancing up at the elder knight, "do you believe in the afterlife?"

"Of course. We all believe in the next world, don't we?"

"I suppose. Do you remember the Tal'mar? The people on the Iron Horse with pointed ears?"

"Sure," Gavin said with a shrug. "Strange bunch. Very quiet."

"They believe their ancestors watch over them. I think they believe they remain here, in this world. That they're... *changed,* but still here. Invisible, I suppose."

"So?"

Kale tossed the charred toy back into the ashes and turned, staring at Gavin. "So what if they're right? What if we don't go to the next world? What if we stay here?"

"Why? What's got you so worried about it?"

Kale frowned. "I saw something earlier. A little boy. Not just saw, I also heard him. He spoke to me. He asked me where his mother was. But the instant I moved, he vanished."

"A ghost?"

Kale didn't answer. They stared at each other, the word hanging in the air between them. Gavin straightened in his saddle, leaning back against the scrolled copper cantle. The leather padding creaked as he moved.

"Don't get too worked up about it. You're not the first man who's seen something that wasn't there. A few mugs of sour ale and you'll wake up swearing you've been to the next world and back."

"I hadn't been drinking," Kale said. "And I know what I saw. I just don't know what it meant."

"And you'll never know. That's the nature of such things. The only certainty is that no one here gets out alive. Just ask the people who lived in this village. They know the answer, but you won't find out until you join them. Anybody who tells you different is either lying or has the *sight*. Good luck proving which."

"I can't stop thinking about him. He seemed so real... so confused. I'm not afraid to die, but I don't want to be confused like that."

"Maybe it takes a while to realize you're dead," said Gavin. "Or, maybe it wasn't a child at all. Maybe it was something else. Just a... a *memory* of him."

"How is that possible?"

"This world is more than just earth and sky, boy. You know that. You've seen the energy in things. You can feel it. I know you can."

Kale thought of Burk, and of how the starfall had changed the man. He wasn't sure if that was what Gavin meant by *energy*, but he had heard Socrates refer to it just so on many occasions. He also knew there were other kinds of energy: the energy in a coil of wire inside the Iron Horse's crude generator, the energy in a seed springing forth from the earth, the energy inside a man that vanished when the light went out in his eyes.

Kale didn't get a chance to elaborate on the question, because at that moment, Sir Hector came galloping up on his dark blue charger. "We've found the trail," the knight said. "It leads into the woods, south of town."

Kale hurried out of the ruins and climbed onto his black warhorse. Hector took off at a gallop and they hurried after him, racing down the main street of Ravenwood. They reached the path shortly, and found Sir Bathus and Sir Flynn waiting.

"Looks like an old hunting trail," Gavin remarked.

"That's fresh blood," Hector said, pointing at a few drops among the ferns at the edge of the path.

Kale heeled his mount to a trot, moving around the others as he headed down the narrow trail. Tree branches slapped at him, but Kale paid no mind. His eyes were focused on the ground.

It was difficult to make their way down the narrow trail; harder still to pick out the random drops of blood along the way. They moved at a slow pace, following the markings deep into the woods, up and down ravines, across a stream, and finally came to a section of dense, shadowy forest. A heavy silence lay upon the place, and the ancient gnarled trees seemed to leer down at them.

"These woods are haunted," Hector said under his breath. "I've heard many legends of demons and witches that live here."

Kale heard a low moaning sound in the distance, and he followed it away from the trail. The others went reluctantly after him. The sound came again, and Hector flinched. The others exchanged uneasy glances.

"What kind of demons were they?" Flynn said, his wide eyes scanning the dark woods. "Can they fly?"

"Not demons," Gavin said, pointing up into the boughs of a twisted old oak. "River reeds."

They followed his gaze and saw a handful of reeds tied into a sort of wind chime that was hanging in the branches. The reeds had been cut and carved into simple flutes, so that each produced a distinct tone as the breeze blew through them.

"Somebody doesn't want us here," Hector said.

"We must be on the right track," said Kale. "Keep moving."

They rode on for a few more minutes, passing through a small orchard, and came to a clearing with an old stone farmhouse with a thatched roof. Nearby stood a dilapidated old barn, and between the two, a garden overgrown with weeds. Scattered around the

JAMIE SEDGWICK

property, they saw the missing heads of the townsfolk fixed onto posts.

"Devils!" Gavin cursed, his gaze fixed on one of the leering faces. "Who would do such a thing?"

"This place is an abomination," Hector said. "We must burn it down!"

Kale held up a hand. "Wait!" he commanded. He turned his steed, taking it all in. A *click-clicking* sound came from the horse's flanks as it turned, and it blew a puff of smoke out through its nostrils. Kale fixed his gaze on the farmhouse. "Hello, there!" he called out. "Is anyone inside?"

He watched the shutters and the door, listening for any sound. His gaze flitted to the dilapidated old barn. One of the doors hung open, but it was dark inside. He leaned close to Gavin and lowered his voice. "Check the barn," he said, nodding in that direction. "Take Flynn with you."

Gavin gestured for the younger knight to join him, and they moved off. Kale turned his attention back to the house. "This is your last chance! You have five seconds to come out before we burn this farm to the ground. Five... Four..."

They heard the clunking sound of the door being unbarred. The rusted old hinges creaked as it slowly swung open. A sixteen-year-old girl appeared, dressed in simple leathers and tall boots, wearing a long green hooded cloak. In her hand she held a longbow with an arrow nocked and ready.

"Who are you?" she said, looking them up and down.

"My name is Kale, First Knight to Queen Aileen of Dragonwall and Commander of the Danaise Militia. These are my men, Sir Hector and Sir Bathus, and over there, by your barn, are Flynn and Gavin. Who are you?"

"My name is Erin, daughter of Malbus and Avery Huntsman. You should have come here when we asked. You are too late."

Gavin and Flynn returned at that moment. "Just a few hens in the barn," the older knight said, drawing his horse alongside Kale's. "And a few fresh graves out back. I'd say this girl has some explaining to do."

"We came as soon as we received your message," Kale said to Erin. "What happened here?"

"Raiding parties. The first time we fought them off, but after that, there were too many. It was an army of ghouls, and it was a slaughter."

"Ghouls?"

"Undead," she said. "The murdered corpses of men, resurrected to fight as soldiers."

Sir Gavin leaned close to Kale, lowering his voice. "Her words don't track," he said under his breath. "I mean yes, ghouls, we've all seen or heard of them, but the rest of it doesn't make sense. No one can control those things. They can't be turned into soldiers."

"You're wrong," said Erin, glaring at him. "I suppose it doesn't matter. We'll all be dead soon, anyway."

"Why the heads?" Kale said, nodding at a nearby post.

"It confuses the undead the ghouls leave behind. They only attack the living."

The sun was shining down on Kale's armor, and he had begun to sweat. A gust of wind blew through the clearing, filling his nostrils with the scent of death. Nearby, flies buzzed around the piked heads. His gaze strayed to the dark woods around them, and a cold chill crawled down his spine. It was an eerie sensation, that cool chill in the hot afternoon sun.

"I think our watcher is back," he said to Gavin in a low voice. The others heard as well, and they all began scanning the woods.

"Then we know it wasn't her."

Kale turned his attention back to Erin. "How did you survive the raid?"

"I was out hunting," she said, holding up her bow. "By the time I returned, the raiders had already done their worst. I came upon a small detachment of ghouls in the woods outside Ravenwood. After killing them, I went home and found…" her gaze went distant and her voice trailed off.

"I'm sorry," Kale said. "We came as fast as we could."

"Not fast enough. You should go now. It's not safe for you to be here. You're putting us all in danger."

"First, I want you to tell me where to find these ghouls."

Her eyes narrowed. "That's a fool's request. You rubes think you can face an army of monsters? You wouldn't survive a minute. I won't send you to your death, even if your apathy did doom my kinsmen to theirs."

"Can't you see we're knights?" Flynn scolded her with an angry glare. "We don't fear the dead."

"Then you are stupid."

Flynn moved to dismount, but Kale stayed him with a wave of his hand. It wouldn't do to have Flynn correcting the girl. Not if they wanted her to cooperate. Not when Flynn needed the same, if not more so. Haughty as he was, Kale knew Flynn was merely acting his age, which wasn't much more than that of the young woman. He remembered being that age. It seemed distant now, almost a different lifetime...

"Erin, you know these woods better than anyone," Kale said. "If these ghouls have an army like you say they do, we should be able to view it from a distance. That should be safe enough. And we'll pay you for your trouble."

Kale pulled a silver coin out of the purse on his belt and flipped it in her direction. Erin snatched it out of the air and held it between her thumb and forefinger, staring at it. It vanished up her sleeve.

"All right," she said. "For three more. If the ghouls find us, you're on your own."

"Two more," Kale said. "And I don't pay you the rest until you show us this army."

She bit her lower lip, glancing back and forth between Kale and Gavin. "It's too far to walk. I'll need a ride."

"Make room," Kale said to Flynn.

The younger knight glared, but he knew better than to openly defy his commander twice in the same day. Flynn still had a swollen cheek, a fat lip, and a bad limp from their earlier encounter. He made room for Erin to climb up behind his saddle.

"Leave the bow," he grumbled as she struggled to get the thing strapped over her shoulders. "You don't need it."

"It goes where I go," she said.

"What's a girl need a bow for? You've got five knights here to protect you."

Erin leaned closer, putting her face close to his. "How much protection is a knight with a fat lip? Is that from the last woman you disrespected?"

Kale grinned as he watched the two sniping at each other. They reminded Kale of how he and River had been, once upon a time... Of course, they had been young then, and he had believed he could somehow make her love him. Kale had accepted reality since then. It was time to give up on that dream.

"Which way?" he said.

Erin pointed the limb of her bow at a trail in the woods south of the farm. Kale narrowed his eyebrows. "South? I was told the Firelands weren't a threat."

"You were told wrong," she said.

Kale and Gavin exchanged a glance. Gavin shifted, his saddle creaking under his weight. "You're sure, lass? I've seen those lands, and there's nothing there but fire and ash. Not even scrub brush."

"If you're afraid, maybe you should stay here," Erin snapped.

Gavin grinned and shook his head. "Move out," Kale said, guiding his mount past the farmhouse.

They moved at a quick pace for several hours, first riding deeper into the woods southwest of the village, and then gradually climbing up into the mountains along the kingdom's southern border. By early evening, the terrain had become increasingly uneven, and their steeds lost their footing several times. Their progress became slow and plodding.

Two hours later, they stopped next to a stream for a quick meal of cold meat and bread. It was dark and chilly, but they had no time for a fire, and there was nowhere to sit except on the hard, rocky ground. They ate in silence, fully alert with the memory of the things they had seen in Ravenwood. They kept their weapons close at hand and their wits sharp. Twenty minutes later, they were back in their saddles and once again climbing.

At last, the clouds parted and the moon's pale light shone down, revealing the line of black cliffs off to their left. Kale called for a halt. He turned in the saddle, examining their surroundings. The air was cool now, filled with the scent of baking evergreen needles and some other evasive scent that reminded him of sulfur. The wilderness off to his right was an ocean of black treetops, the peaks of the tallest trees thrusting up into the sky, silver starlight glinting off the branches.

"How much farther?" Kale said, turning to face Erin.

She leaned out from behind Flynn, scanning the terrain ahead of them. "Just a few more miles. There's a path between the cliffs up ahead, but it's a steep climb."

"We'll leave the chargers here," Kale said. "They can't handle this rough terrain."

Gavin sighed. "It's for the best, I suppose. If we wanted to go much farther, we'd have to rewind these horses by hand."

"I didn't know that was possible," said Kale.

"It's possible, but it's not a job you want to do. You have to run a long iron bar through the key, and get three or four men pulling on it at once. Very carefully, of course."

"Is it dangerous?"

Gavin gave him a grim smile. "When I was a child, I saw two men trying to wind a horse without any help. One of them lost his grip on the pipe. It broke his arm, and crushed his partner's skull. Then the pipe got loose and shot out of the keyhole like a bullet. Embedded itself so deep in a wood post that it's still there today."

"Let's not do that," Kale said, dismounting.

The others climbed off their horses and Erin moved to the front of the line. "This way," she said, starting to climb the path. "Keep moving or it'll take all night."

Flynn leaned close to Hector and whispered, "Looks like we've got a new commander."

"She's got guts, I'll give her that," Hector replied.

The trail narrowed as they climbed, and it became progressively difficult to pick out the path in the shadows of the cliffs. Gavin stumbled more than once, and Kale was beginning to worry about the elderly man. He was tempted to say something, but was unsure about how to broach the subject without hurting his friend's feelings.

The path straightened out then, and a small meadow-like clearing opened up to their left at the base of the cliffs. A tiny stream ran down the face of the cliffs, creating bubbling waterfalls here and there before it cascaded into a pool at the bottom.

"This is the place," Erin said. "We have to climb the cliffs here. This stream is safe to drink. You should refill your canteens."

The knights followed her advice, except for Flynn, who stood back waiting impatiently. "You should drink," Erin urged him. "The climb ahead is difficult."

"I'm not thirsty," Flynn said.

"Then at least fill your canteen."

He held it up. "It's still full. I don't need to drink every ten minutes, like these old warhorses."

"Who you callin' old?" Gavin said, wiping the sweat from his forehead with a damp rag. "I'm in the prime of my life. Just give me a quick nap, and then I'll straighten you out."

Erin laughed and Flynn couldn't help cracking a smile. Kale, who had been kneeling at the stream, attached his replenished canteen to the hook on his belt as he rose to his feet. He approached the cliffs, gazing up the slick stone face.

"We start here, in the waterfall," Erin said, pointing to a ledge in the stone. "From there, the path moves to the left, toward that cleft up there."

Kale followed with his eyes as she pointed the way. When he saw the degree of difficulty in the climb, he turned to the group and said, "I don't think we all need to go. Flynn, you're with me. The rest of you wait here."

"Hang on now," said Gavin. "I was only joking about that nap."

"I know that, but it's a steep climb and the more people we have up that cliff, the greater the chances of something going wrong. Besides, if we have to leave in a hurry, it'll be better with fewer of us scrambling down those rocks."

Gavin glanced at Hector and Bathus. None of the three seemed happy about the decision. They had all been looking forward to seeing this so-called army of ghouls.

"I say Gavin should stay," said Bathus. "After all, he is our elder, and therefore deserving the most respect... but not the rest of us."

"Respect," Gavin spat. "What's that got to do with it? You're not even making sense."

"He thinks you're senile as well," Flynn said, grinning at them.

"You're not helping," Kale snapped. "My decision is made. Flynn and I will scout ahead. The rest of you stay on guard and make sure no one cuts off our escape."

"Aye, aye, Commander," Gavin said in a cynical tone. Kale ignored him. He crawled onto the ledge at the lowest level of the waterfall. The cold water splashed over his boots and the legs of his breeches while he searched for his next handhold. As he was looking, Erin scurried up the ledge next to him and went racing past. Kale watched her as she leapt agilely from ledge to outcropping and back again, moving from side to side as she scaled the sheer face of the cliff. She paused a few seconds later to look down at them.

"Are you coming?" she said.

Kale heard the others chuckling behind him. "Maybe you should stay down here with us, old timer," said Gavin. Kale snorted, and started to climb.

Erin made it to the top in less than a minute, but it took Kale and Flynn considerably longer. Kale told himself his armor and heavy weapons slowed him down, but a nagging voice in the back of his head pointed out that Flynn was right on his heels all the way up. The difficult truth was that his youth was behind him, and the sheer rock face was a painful reminder of that fact.

Near the top, Kale reached for a rock that gave way as soon as he put some weight on it. His hand slipped, and the rock went tumbling down.

"Watch out!" he called out, but it was already too late. The rock struck Flynn on the forehead, leaving a long gash. The young knight grunted as blood began to flow from the wound.

"Are you all right?" Kale said.

"Fine," Flynn growled. "Just keep moving."

Kale pulled himself over the ledge and rose to his feet. He found himself standing on a broad plateau a hundred yards across. The moon stood behind him, and the sky to the south was dark. A shadow seemed to cover the land. Kale heard Flynn grunting behind him, and he bent over to offer the young knight a hand. Flynn ignored the offer, and finished the climb without assistance.

"Over here," Erin said, standing near the southern ledge.

The two knights joined her. They found themselves standing at the edge of a two thousand foot drop straight down. The land below was dark, illuminated here and there by the orange glow of volcanic rivers. A warm breeze washed over them, and Kale nearly gagged on the stench of sulfur and burning tar. His eyes watered and his lungs burned, but he stood unmoving, scanning the terrain.

"There," Erin said, pointing to the southwest. Kale looked, and saw nothing but barren, volcanic land. Then he realized that something was moving down there. He moved along the edge of the cliff, searching for a better perspective. As his eyes adjusted, he began to separate form from shadow. There were figures down there, moving in the darkness, he realized. People. And something tall, some sort of tower, perhaps.

"I'd kill for River's scope right now," he said.

"Hector has one," said Flynn.

Kale turned to Erin. "Would you mind? You're the fastest."

"No problem," she said, "but it'll cost you extra. Speaking of which, you haven't paid me yet."

She held out her palm. Kale rolled his eyes. He opened his purse and counted out three more silver coins, and a copper. Erin made them disappear, and then she hurried back towards the cliff.

A silence fell over the two knights as they stood waiting. Kale thought perhaps he should say something to Flynn, that he should find some way to make things right between them. On the other hand, Flynn had decided to challenge Kale's authority, not the other way around. As much as Kale wanted to be friends with the other knights, he knew that first and foremost it was his job to make them obey and respect him. If they couldn't do that, then ultimately they would have to abandon their positions, or find a way to remove Kale from his. That would be easier said than done. He was getting pretty good at watching his back.

Erin returned, interrupting his thoughts. She handed Kale the scope and he stretched it out to full length. He put it to his eye and zeroed in on the area they had been watching. Somehow, the lenses of the scope almost seemed to magnify the starlight, giving him a brighter, sharper view of the scene than he had expected.

Kale's jaw dropped, and his face paled. He lowered the scope. "We have to go," he said. "We have to go, right now!"

"What is it?" said Flynn. "Let me see!"

Flynn reached for the scope, but at that moment, they heard a shout coming from behind them.

"Ambush!" Gavin cried out from the bottom of the cliff.

Chapter 9

Kale scrambled over the ledge. His movements were reckless and uninformed in the darkness, but he somehow managed to move from ledge to outcropping without falling and breaking his neck. Emboldened by his success, and overcome with the battle frenzy, he put on a burst of speed.

Kale moved left and right, zigzagging down the face of the cliff. He latched onto a stone and lowered himself to this next handhold. Putting his weight all on one foot, he caught a ledge of sharp stone that protruded out of the cliff wall. As he shifted his weight, the stone gave way. It went out from under him, and the sudden weight ripped his hands free. Kale went tumbling wildly down the face of the cliff.

Stars and darkness flashed through his vision. The wind rushed in his ears. He struck an outcropping and bounced off. The motion sent him tumbling sideways, spinning out of control. His head swam, and he closed his eyes, waiting for the inevitable crash at the bottom. Death was but a fraction of a second away.

Something struck him full-on across the chest, driving his breath from his lungs in a loud *oomf!* Branches slapped at his face. He felt an unmistakable length of a juniper's trunk beneath him, slowly bending under his weight. Instinctively, the warrior latched onto the tree with both hands and held on for dear life.

His full weight came to bear, and the roots creaked as they strained to support him. His gaze darted left and right, searching for another handhold to latch onto before the tree collapsed. In the pale moonlight, he saw a sharp stone angled out of the sheer cliff face less than two yards off. Just out of reach, but if he could stretch a little...

At that moment, the juniper's roots gave way. The trunk yanked free of the stone, and Kale went tumbling. Almost instantaneously, the twenty-foot freefall ended in a catastrophic landing. He heard a grunt and felt the unmistakable crack of bones as someone broke his fall. The air rushed from his lungs and Kale thrashed, struggling to refill them. The world spun. Dark shapes loomed over him. He saw flashes of silver in the moonlight, heard the cries of battle, and the sounds of ringing steel.

Kale rolled off the broken body beneath him, and clambered to his knees. His breath came in shallow gasps. His broken rib screamed with every inhalation. He could make nothing of the body next to him in the darkness, save that the man was almost certainly dead. Kale prayed it wasn't one of his companions. He pushed to his feet, drawing one of the two-handed swords from the baldric on his back.

"There!" a voice shouted. It was Gavin. Kale saw the knight's shadowy figure pointing across the clearing. He drew his gaze in that direction and saw a dark shape lumbering at the base of the cliff. Kale shook off his pain, and rushed to meet the attacker.

As he closed in on the figure, it heard him coming. The creature turned on him with an animalistic snarl and Kale froze, sword held high in the air. The moonlight fell across the creature's horrific, decaying face. Chunks of rotting flesh revealed a hollow opening under its cheekbone and around the left eye. Somehow, the organ remained in place, swiveling madly in its broken socket. A brass hinge held the jaw in place, gleaming under the starlight.

It lunged at him, fingers outstretched, claw-like nails groping for his throat. Kale let out a horrified gasp as he pushed the ghoul's arms away. It latched onto his left arm and snapped at him like a crazed animal. The ghoul's rotten teeth clamped down on his vambrace, and Kale heard the *shrieking* noise of broken teeth sliding across hardened steel.

He shook his arm, trying to free himself from the creature's grip, but it held fast, clinging to him like an iron vice. With a look of absolute revulsion, Kale brought down the pommel of his sword on the ghoul's head. The decaying skull shattered, exposing rotting brain matter and black, coagulated blood. The ghoul relaxed its grip, and Kale fell back a step. With a flick of his wrist, his blade flashed across the creature's throat. The decapitated skull rolled off to the side as the body collapsed in front of him.

Kale heard a shout and spun to see Erin standing on a boulder at the base of the cliff. She released an arrow and it flew past him, embedding itself deep into the chest of another attacker. He stepped sideways, bringing the tip of his sword upward through the creature's jaw. The point of his blade erupted through the top of the ghoul's skull. As he withdrew the blade, the creature crumpled to the ground. The axe in its hands clattered across the stones.

Flynn let out a war cry as he closed in on another of the ghouls. It fought back with the perfection of a trained professional, parrying his blows and countering with equally measured skill. This ghoul was large, taller than Flynn, and much stronger. It wore several pieces of plate armor, and Kale saw the glint of moonlight on the metal in its joints, holding them in place.

The creature bore down on Flynn with a series of powerful overhead strokes, driving the young knight back step by step. As the blows rained down, Kale saw Flynn's grip loosening on the sword. The ghoul noticed, too. It grinned, an eerie hideous smile that sent a chill crawling down Kale's spine. He broke into a sprint, but knew he'd never make it in time.

Flynn dropped to his knees as the ghoul raised its weapon for the final blow. As the blade came down, Flynn lifted the blade with both hands in what appeared to be a last-ditch attempt to block the attack. Instead of blocking, he twisted the handle, activating a hidden mechanism inside the hilt. The sword's blade separated from the fittings with a loud *Snap!* It shot forward, piercing the ghoul's chest plate, and drove deep into the monster's chest. The blade protruded through the ghoul's back, gleaming in the moonlight, streaked with inky black blood.

The force of the blow drove the creature back a step and Flynn rolled away. At the same instant, they heard the *twang* of a bowstring and an arrow pierced the monster's eye. The creature swayed, reaching for the feathered vanes projecting from its eye socket. Kale arrived, beheading the ghoul with a sweep of his blade. The fiend crumpled.

Kale stood over Flynn, looking down at him. The young knight was bruised and bleeding, but seemed otherwise in good health.

"Thanks," Flynn said. "He almost had me."

"Nonsense," Kale said. He reached out, helping Flynn to his feet. "You had him right where you wanted him."

Kale drew the second sword from his baldric and handed it to Flynn. A few yards back, Erin cleared her throat.

"Never mind me," she said with a glare. "I didn't save your lives just now or anything."

"Agreed," Kale said with a wry grin. Erin narrowed her eyebrows and started to say something, but the two knights were already rejoining the battle. She snorted as she nocked another arrow.

In the darkness and confusion, it was difficult to determine which bodies were those of the attackers and which were friends. The knights called out to each other, trying to identify themselves in the chaos. More than once, Kale found himself crossing swords with a new opponent only to suddenly recognize the helm or armor of one of his companions.

Erin lit a torch and threw it across the clearing, into the midst of the battle. *Clever,* Kale thought as the flickering light fell on the faces of their attackers. He found himself next to a tall knight wearing dark-colored armor. The armor looked like Hector's, but the knight spun on him with a snarl. Before he could raise his blade, the ghoul punched him in the face with a gauntleted fist. Stars flashed in his vision, and he stumbled back a step.

The ghoul closed in, horrific dead eyes glaring with hatred, a patchwork of bronze gears *click-clicking* on the side of its face. The clockwork monster raised its sword -a bastard sword with a jewel-encrusted hilt- and brought the blade down in a sweeping arc. Kale parried the attack. He stepped in to counter with a strike to the abdomen, but his blade glanced harmlessly off the undead knight's armor. The ghoul took another wide swing at him. Kale blocked, countered, and the ghoul did the same.

Kale pressed on, ignoring the sharp stabbing pain in his midsection and the horrified sense that he couldn't believe what he was seeing. Everything Kale thought he knew about the undead had suddenly changed. These creatures, these ghouls, could *fight*. They were intelligent; dangerous. In fact, Kale had his hands full just keeping his attacker's sword at bay. No matter how fast he swung, or how he countered, the creature always had a response.

Kale fought the fatigue that threatened to slow his defenses. *Just a bit longer,* he thought. *If I can hold him off a bit longer...*

No sooner had he thought it, than the tip of Hector's sword exploded through the undead knight's chest. The creature froze, eyes wide with surprise, sword still raised for the next blow. Kale capitalized on the moment. He decapitated the ghoul in one smooth slice. The creature collapsed between them, the mechanical gearworks in its face clicking wildly.

The two knights locked eyes. Kale opened his mouth to speak but Hector raised his sword and shouted, "Step aside!"

Kale instinctively obeyed, and barely avoided Hector's flashing blade as it thrust toward his midsection. Another ghoul seemed to materialize out of the darkness, and Hector's blade plunged into its chest. The creature dropped to its knees. Up ahead, they heard Gavin shouting:

"They're retreating! They're retreating!"

Hector beheaded the ghoul. The two knights hurried up the trail towards Gavin, stepping over the bodies littering their path. They found the elderly knight twenty yards up the slope, leaning on the handle of his sword. The remaining ghouls had disappeared up the slope.

Kale wiped the blood from his blade and sheathed it. He took a deep breath, and a shockwave of pain went through his body. He doubled over, hands on his knees, sucking in shallow gasps.

"You all right?" Hector said.

"Just... my ribs," Kale said as he tried to catch his breath. "I'm fine. You?"

"A few bruises."

Kale stood upright, adjusting his armor so it wouldn't press against his tender ribcage. "Have you ever seen anything like that?" he said. "Ghouls wearing armor, fighting with swords?"

"Never," said Gavin. "I've seen undead before, but never like this."

"Nor I," said Hector. "According to all the stories I've heard, these creatures are supposed to be mindless; barely even alive at all."

"We need to inform the queen," Kale said. "These incursions are just the beginning."

He turned, looking over the group. They all had injuries -cuts, bruises, a few open wounds- except for Erin. She alone seemed to have escaped unscathed. Sir Bathus moaned. He had come up the path behind them and now stood at the back of the group with a hand held over his side. Blood flowed freely between his gauntleted fingers. Kale took a step in his direction, and Bathus dropped to his knees.

"Give me a hand," Kale said to the others. "Get him to the clearing."

Together, they lifted the knight and carried him back down the trail, reclining him gently on the moss at the edge of the pool.

"What happened?" Kale said as he pulled Bathus's hand away to reveal the wound.

"Hard to say. Too much going on in the dark. I guess one of them got me with his pigsticker."

"I need to remove your chest plate," Kale said.

Bathus leaned forward so Kale could reach the buckles. The knight winced, and a moan escaped his lips. Kale loosened the straps and pulled the plate over Bathus's head. He bent closer, examining the wound. "I need more light," he said.

Erin collected the torch she'd left on the trail, She hurried over with it, holding it above their heads. Kale's expression darkened as he got a good look at the injury. "This wound is deep. We need to get you back to Dragonwall."

"I can help," Erin said. She opened her bag and rummaged around. She produced a small tin, which she opened to reveal some sort of brown jelly-like substance.

"What is that?" Bathus said. His voice rattled as he spoke.

"It's a salve. It will clean the wound and staunch the bleeding." Erin ripped a shred of cloth from the end of her cloak. She covered it in salve and then pressed it to the wound. "There," she said. "Hold it tight. Keep pressure on it... and drink this." She handed him a small flask. Bathus took a sip, and his eyes brightened as the liquid touched his lips. A weak grin spread across his face.

"That's booze!" he said cheerfully.

"Yes, it will slow the infection in your gut. Drink it all. Drink it fast."

"That, I can do." Bathus tilted his head back and emptied the flask. He handed it back to her and wiped the moisture from his beard with the back of his gauntlet. Kale rose to his feet and surveyed the rest of the group.

"Where is Flynn?" he said. The others turned, scanning the darkened path and the woods down the slope.

"I don't see him," said Hector. "If he'd fallen down the hill there, we'd see tracks."

"Here!" Gavin said. He had walked up the path a ways, and he came back into the light carrying Kale's second sword. "They must've taken him."

Kale cursed under his breath. "Hector, I need you to get Bathus back to Dragonwall. When you get there, inform the queen of our situation. Tell her I'll be back as soon as I can. Tell her to activate the militia."

Hector's eyes widened, and Gavin cleared his throat. "Kale, what exactly did you see beyond that cliff?"

Kale didn't answer, but the look on his face was answer enough. Gavin rolled his eyes heavenward. Hector groaned. He began pacing back and forth along the trail.

"I didn't believe it. I thought it was just a girl's fantasy, but it's not." He turned to face them. "How can it be? Where did they come from?"

"I told you!" Erin said, crossing her arms over her chest and scowling at him. "And I'm *not* a little girl."

Hector ignored her comment. "What do we do now?" he said. "How do we fight an army like that? How do you fight an army that's already dead?"

Kale waved his arm with a dismissive gesture. "We don't have time for this. Take Bathus back to Dragonwall and give the queen my message. Dispatch a messenger to the Iron Horse. Tell Socrates he has to turn back. They shouldn't go anywhere near the Firelands."

"What about her?" Gavin said, nodding at Erin.

"What do you mean?" she said, squaring her shoulders.

"It's not safe at that farm. Not with these ghouls around."

"I'm going with Kale to rescue Flynn."

Kale shook his head. "Don't be ridiculous. You've seen these things up close. They're dangerous."

Erin leaned against her longbow and gave him a cocky smile. "So am I. In fact, it seems to me that I'm the only who came out of that fight in one piece. Look at the rest of you! You look like you got steamrolled."

"She has a point," Gavin said. "She's good with that bow."

"I'm also the only one who knows her way around these mountains," Erin said. "I can show you the pass. You'll never find it on your own."

Kale sighed. "Fine. The three of us, then." He grabbed Bathus by the shoulders and helped him back to his feet. Hector took over, throwing the knight's arm over his shoulder to help him walk back to the chargers. Kale turned back to Gavin and Erin.

"Let's get moving," he said. "There's no telling what those things will do to Flynn if we give them the chance."

Chapter 10

As Shayla regained consciousness, she became aware of cold, damp stones beneath her. She heard water dripping and noticed the metallic scent of blood in the air. She recognized another scent, mingling with the wet-animal odor of the elk hide cloak over her shoulders. The scent was familiar, but she didn't have a name for it. Somehow, she couldn't place it.

The pale green light emanating from the fountain seemed oddly bright. She remembered the glow of starfall -had seen it up close more than once- and didn't remember it having this level of luminescence. Then again, this may have been the effect of her eyes adjusting to the pitch-blackness of the cave. Shayla sat upright, and the room spun. Her stomach did flip-flops, and she waited for the spell to pass.

After a few minutes, Shayla rose to her feet and stood there swaying, trying to take inventory of her condition. Her head ached from the base of her skull to the top. Cuts and bruises covered her body. Shayla's dress was torn to shreds, so much so that the last ribbons of fabric fell to the floor as she moved. Her boots were missing as well. They must have fallen off when she was being carried through the tunnels by her attackers.

Shayla covered her nakedness, pulling the cloak tight about her shoulders. She scanned the cave looking for a torch or even a discarded nub of candle; anything to help find her way out of there. She found nothing.

Her stomach rumbled, and she wondered how long she had been down there. Had she slept through the night? Longer, perhaps? It didn't matter. She had to get moving, had to get her blood flowing. She needed to get warm and dry before she caught a fever.

Shayla took a few uncertain steps into the tunnel, blinking against the darkness, teeth chattering with cold. The stones felt painful and irregular against her bare feet. She was unaccustomed to walking without boots. Her cloak-shrouded body cast a long shadow in the dim phosphorescent glow of the fountain, and the sound of dripping water echoed maddeningly in her ears.

The tunnel curved right and then left, and began to climb upwards. The light of the fountain faded away behind her. Somehow, Shayla was able to make out certain details of her surroundings even in the darkness. The slope of the floor in front of her, for example, or the jagged stone thrusting out of the tunnel wall. These details were hazy and colorless, but nonetheless recognizable.

Shayla remained aware of the scent of blood lingering in the tunnel, pungent and foreboding, and it occurred to her that this must be from the man she had stabbed during her ordeal. Images flooded her mind: cruel faces leering at her out of the darkness, rough hands forcing her down into the water, the cold burning sensation of drowning, the absolute overwhelming panic...

Shayla closed her eyes and placed a hand against the wall, steadying herself. She could see her attacker's faces. Each and every one. She would never forget them -never forget what they had done to her- but now was not the time to dwell on that. First, she had to get to safety. There would be time for revenge later.

Shayla pushed on, making her way up the tunnel, rising from the womb of the mountain as if it had birthed her in the vast darkness below. Soon, she heard the distant sounds of civilization: the churning, humming noises of machines and motors, the drumming footsteps of men in spring-powered suits hauling loads of ore and equipment up and down the mountain's interior, the ringing sound of anvils and the dull rumble of the lava cauldrons beneath the mountain. Then, eventually, voices. They were distant, muffled, unintelligible.

The tunnel became a passageway, and Shayla followed it until she came to a spot she recognized. It was a narrow hallway near the base of the mountain; a rarely traveled passageway connecting many of the lower tunnels. It was unlikely that anyone would find her here, but still she proceeded with caution. Shayla took the staircase around the next corner, and began the slow hike up the mountain.

As Shayla climbed the stairs, it occurred to her that she was naked, wrapped only in the cloak her attackers had abandoned. It wouldn't do for her to be seen like this. She had a reputation to protect. To the people of Dragonwall, Shayla was a beautiful, exotic stranger - not someone they could trust, perhaps, but someone they longed for, or longed to be. It wouldn't do, allowing them to see her humbled in this manner, stripped down to nothing, bruised and battered, tossed aside like a cheap whore.

That wasn't her only problem. The men who had attacked her were still there, somewhere. They were still in the mountain, and if they knew she had survived, there was no telling what they might do. Logic dictated the best thing to do now was to leave. Shayla couldn't stay in Stormwatch. She was too well known there, and far too likely to encounter the men who had tried to kill her. She needed to find a safe way to escape the mountain.

Shayla paused in her thoughts as she entered the Chamber of Kings and saw her reflection in a full-length polished silver mirror. It was a tall, intricately wrought furnishing made by the highly talented smiths of Dragonwall. The entire chamber was filled with such treasures, all dedicated to the memory of the great kings of the past. Their portraits hung on the wall adjacent to the mirror, but it was the mirror that caught her attention.

Shayla took a step closer, the cloak falling away as she saw her likeness reflected there. She frowned, staring at her naked reflection, perplexed by what she saw.

She had *grown*. That was the first thing she realized. Shayla had always been a woman of average height, like her entire royal line, but somehow she had grown *taller*. There was no doubt about it. She turned, comparing herself to the table and chairs nearby, to the suits of armor near the entrance and the swords hanging on the wall.

Not just that; she was thinner, too. Statuesque. Her beauty remained, but her face... it seemed somehow changed as well. And her ears. Her ears! They had elongated into tiny elfin points, much like those of the Tal'mar. Her eyes widened and she raised a hand to stroke the soft velvety fur that covered them with the tips of her fingers. It was fine, almost transparent except for the golden-tan color that seemed to shimmer in the light. She took a step closer, blinking, studying every detail.

Her eyes seemed unusually dark. As Shayla came face to face with her reflection, she realized that her pupils had changed. They were tiny horizontal slits, surrounded by a mesmerizing pool of swirling gold. The overall shape remained. She looked human enough, but her eyes had become the eyes of.. of what? Some animal. A horse perhaps, or...

Shayla took a step back. She reached out, touching the mirror, somehow doubting the reflection it cast. It couldn't be real. But as her fingertips touched the polished metal, they left hazy circular prints that blocked out her reflection. An involuntary whimper slipped through her lips, the sound trailing off into a mournful wail. Her shoulders shook with sobs, bitter tears streaming down her cheeks. She dropped to her knees, eyes downcast, unable to face the abomination staring back at her.

The fur-lined cloak was on the floor next to her. She reached for it, a curious look sweeping across her features as she held it in both hands. She touched the fabric, the leather, put the fur to her nose and inhaled its scent.

In that breath came a distant recognition, like a long-forgotten memory rising from the depths of her subconscious. She closed her eyes and a vision of the creature appeared before her. It was tall, elegant, wildly powerful. A noble animal, recognized and worshipped for its rugged power and beauty, and sought after by men both as a prized trophy and as a spiritual guide. The cloak was made from the hide of an elk, and somehow, without even being able to explain, Shayla knew that she had become one with that creature. She had somehow absorbed its essence into her own body.

No, not *somehow*. She knew exactly how. It was the starfall that had done it, just as it had done to Burk when he purposely -and insanely- imbibed the fuel. The mutations had been more pronounced in him, because the exposure was more direct and more concentrated. It had turned the blacksmith into a monster, a creature more animal than human.

In either case, the change was permanent. The change was always permanent. Never again would Shayla look upon her reflection and see her true self. She doubled over, weeping into the fur.

Chapter 11

The Iron Horse crewmembers stood agape as the ghoulish overseer approached them. The crew had encountered creatures like Anu-Abas before, but... not exactly. Unlike the living corpses of Blackstone castle, this creature was sentient. It could *talk*. Not only that, but it somehow had the intelligence to augment parts of its own decaying body with mechanical replacements.

Anu-Abas stopped a few yards away, glaring at the crew. Socrates took a few steps closer with his hands held up in a nonthreatening gesture. A few puffs of steam shot out of the ape's exhaust chimney, and his legs made quiet *whirring* and *clicking* noises as he moved. He craned his neck a little, looking up into the tall creature's face. As he moved, the overseer's eyepiece rotated, the lenses twisting back and forth as it focused on him.

"Forgive our intrusion," said the ape. "We are here on an exploratory mission, and we only wish to observe your culture; to become allies with your people. We have often found such relationships may be beneficial to all parties involved. I assure you, we have the utmost respect."

The overseer raised his scepter. He leveled it at Socrates with a menacing scowl, brandishing it like a weapon. Before he could react further, they heard a shout and a loud *crack!* in the distance.

A group of thirty people came walking out of the jungle a few hundred yards away. They were peasants, dressed mostly in rags and ranging in age from five or six to seventy. They were filthy, their hair caked with mud, blisters and welts marring their skin. Some carried baskets brimming with clusters of bright red grapes, while others pulled two-wheeled handcarts that were also loaded down with the fruit.

Another overseer rode alongside them in a two-wheeled chariot. He was tall like the first, and he brandished a whip in his right hand. His body was mostly intact, with the exception of a mechanical gauntlet that had replaced his left hand.

River stared at the chariot, trying to figure out the means of propulsion. She did not hear any engine, or see any exhaust. Perhaps, she thought, it was electrical, like the motor they had recovered from the crashed train. Unfortunately, she couldn't be sure without a closer look.

The moment they were free of the jungle, one of the children broke away from the group. He was a ten-year-old boy with olive skin and dark curls reaching down to his shoulders. He took off at a run, and the overseer on the chariot shouted a warning. One of the women in the group, likely the boy's mother, cried out and took off after him.

The crew of the Iron Horse watched with a sort of detached confusion. It wasn't immediately apparent what was going on, but it became all too clear as the charioteer raised his metal-handled whip. He whirled it overhead, snapping it in the air with the sound of an exploding firecracker. It struck the woman across her back. She fell to her knees, sobbing, reaching out to the boy, begging him to return. The people around her averted their eyes, shame and fear evident on their faces.

"Socrates!" River said, reaching for her revolver. "These people are slaves!"

"Wait," the ape commanded, raising his hand in the air. "Give me a chance to settle this dispute peacefully."

The charioteer guided his vehicle around the woman and put on a burst of speed in pursuit of the child. The boy darted left and right as he dodged through the pedestrians inside the village. He raced alongside one of the smaller pyramids, and cut across the broad lawn, moving in the direction of the crew. The charioteer called out another warning and then cracked the whip over the boy's head. Terrified, the boy stumbled. He hit the ground and rolled. He immediately pushed back to his feet and broke into a fresh sprint.

By this time, River and the others could see the terror on the poor child's face. His eyes widened a little as he saw them, but he kept running in their direction. Perhaps he sensed that they were like him in some way; that they would protect him from the overseer and his kind. Or, perhaps he simply saw the opportunity to lose his pursuer in the crowd.

The whip cracked again, and this time it struck home. It snapped across the boy's legs. An immediate scream burst forth from his lips, and he fell. He tumbled across the grass and came to a stop sprawled out on his belly. He didn't move after that; he simply lay there, twitching and sobbing.

The charioteer hit the brakes, skidding sideways as he pulled up alongside the child. They were close enough now that his undead features were clear. He had gray-blue skin, slightly darker than the first overseer's icy blue color. He also had a short silver beard, and was missing his nose. The creature's countenance was even more horrifying to look upon than his companion's.

Summoning his courage, the young boy pushed to his feet. He straightened his shoulders and glared up at the charioteer.

"You have had your last warning, boy!"

"Wait!" Socrates called out. "Please, listen to reason-"

The charioteer raised his whip, ignoring the ape's plea. He twisted his wrist, spiraling the weapon expertly overhead.

There was a loud *crack!* and a perfect round hole appeared in the center of the overseer's forehead. His jaw dropped in surprise. The sound of the gunshot echoed through the jungle around them as the whip slipped from his hand. For a moment, everything went silent. No one in the vicinity spoke, or even moved.

The overseer slumped, his dead body toppling over the side of the chariot, and landed on the ground in front of the child. The entire village turned to look at River.

River stood at the front of the crew, her shoulders thrust back defiantly, the revolver still in her hand. A small cloud of compressed air dissipated as it drifted up from the barrel.

"Fool!" shouted Anu-Abas. "How dare you?"

He stepped past Socrates, brandishing his scepter. Thane moved to block the overseer's path, and the creature thrust the scepter into the bard's midsection. There was a lightning-like *crackle* and Thane's eyes went wide. His body shook uncontrollably for a second and then dropped to the ground shaking and lurching.

Loren had an arrow nocked, and he let it loose. It sang through the air, penetrating the overseer's chest armor and passing all the way through. Anu-Abas grinned. He leveled his weapon at the Tal'mar warrior and squeezed the handle. There was another arcing sound as an invisible energy field drove Loren, Kynan, and Micah to the ground simultaneously. The concussive energy struck River as well, but she was at the edge of the field and managed to stay on her feet. She raised her revolver to fire again, but Anu-Abas was a half-second faster.

The overseer adjusted his weapon's aim and released another blast. With a crackling *buzz,* it swept River off her feet and threw her back several yards. The revolver tumbled from her grip as she landed in the grass, flat on her back. Socrates leapt forward, catching Anu-Abas by the arm. He yanked the overseer off-balance, and the ghoul dropped his weapon. Micah scurried in to snatch it up.

Anu-Abas took a swing at Socrates, and the ape's head made a dull clanging noise as the overseer's fist struck home. It was a powerful blow, but not enough to jar Socrates. The mechanical simian reached out, catching the overseer by the scruff of his neck. He slammed the overseer's face down into his hardened steel kneecap with the sound of a smashing melon.

Before Anu-Abas could recover, Socrates lifted him in the air and threw him to the ground. The overseer landed heavily on his back. The violent attack would have killed any normal man, but Anu-Abas was hardly phased. He rolled over and started crawling to his knees. As he moved, Micah rushed in and jammed the scepter into the overseer's face. Anu-Abas shook and convulsed until Micah lowered the weapon. The overseer collapsed, and went entirely still. The others came closer, gazing down at the ghoul.

"Is he still alive?" Micah said, glancing at Socrates.

"Alive? That's not the word I would use." He knelt down, the gears inside his body whirring as he reached out to touch Anu-Abas on the throat. "He has no pulse, but that may not indicate anything. The brain and nervous system-"

Before he could finish his thought, they heard a horrendous scream in the direction of the largest pyramid. They all turned to see a third overseer at the base of the structure. This creature wore a kilt of gold and silver, with a matching cloak. Long jet-black hair hung down over his shoulders. He appeared younger than the first two, or at least in better physical condition. There were no mechanical replacement parts or augmentations that they could see.

The ghoul rushed the group, barehanded and snarling like a rabid dog. The crewmembers spread out, giving themselves the room to fight. River lifted her revolver and lined up the sights.

"I can't get a shot," she said. "There are too many people behind him."

"Same here," Loren grumbled.

As the overseer broke into a sprint, a gray-haired man split away from the crowd and ran straight at him. The ghoul was oblivious to this, until the man crashed into him, tackling the overseer to the ground. They landed hard on the grass and started to grapple. Somehow, the slave managed to get up on top of the ghoul. He started swinging at the overseer, raining blows down on his face and chest.

A cry went up among the other slaves. They converged, rushing in to attack the fallen overseer. They kicked and stomped with their bare feet, and smashed him with sticks and rocks. The creature cried out as the crowd closed in around him. The screams went on for a few seconds and then abruptly died.

Socrates rushed forward, pushing his way through the crowd. By the time he made it to the fallen overseer, there was very little recognizable of the creature. The ghoul's decomposing flesh had fallen off in many places, exposing raw white bone. His neck was twisted at a sharp angle, and his skull was crushed into the ground like an overripe fruit.

"Get back," Socrates said. "That's enough. The overseer is dead."

The slaves glared at him, unable to comprehend his words, apparently uncertain as to whether he was an ally or another overseer. One of them smacked him across the back with the handle of a hoe. The handle snapped in two, and the ape's back made a loud metal *clanging* noise. Socrates turned on him with a snarl, and the slave dropped the broken hoe and fled.

"Are there more?" Socrates shouted at others. The slaves stared back at him stupidly. "O-ver-seers," the ape said, pronouncing the syllables slowly and deliberately as he pointed at their fallen enemy. "Are there more?"

"No more," said a voice behind him.

Socrates turned and saw the old slave who had attacked the overseer. He was sitting on the stairs at the base of one of the smaller pyramids. He was stooped over, still struggling to catch his breath. His thin robes were torn, his tattered clothes revealing long angry gashes and bruises across his arms and chest.

Whip-scars covered nearly every inch of his exposed skin. The scars even marred the old man's sandaled feet.

Socrates approached him. "Are you all right?" he said.

The old man wrinkled up his face. "No, I am not. You killed us, machine. We all will die because of you."

Socrates frowned, looking his accuser up and down. "I tried to avoid this, I'm sure you can see that."

"Bah!" The man made a sweeping gesture. "By killing *three*? When the others come for the harvest, we will be meat for the birds!"

"Others?" Socrates said. He heard a noise behind him, and realized that the rest of the crew had come up to stand behind him. The old man saw Micah among them, and his eyebrows went up.

"Are you a trickster?" he said with childlike awe.

Micah approached him, pulling off his wide-brimmed hat to reveal his imp-like features. He had started growing a short goatee, which made his long, sharply pointed chin seem even longer. "My name is Micah. I'm the train's cartographer. Who are you?"

"They call me Rapa-nu. It is our word for grandfather. I'm the oldest man in the village."

"How old are you, Grandfather?"

"One hundred and three. I have seen many generations, but only one man who was older than me. Still, I am like a child to the Ana-nuit. The gods live forever. Do tricksters live forever?"

"Gods?" Micah said, glancing over his shoulder at Socrates. "You said there were more of them? How many?"

Rapa-nu locked gazes with the halfling. Micah frowned as he saw the careworn look on the man's face, the tiredness in his eyes. He was pitiful. He put a gentle hand on Rapa-nu's shoulder and squeezed reassuringly.

"Don't fear," he said in a quiet voice. "We can help you. Look at my friends, look at their weapons! They can kill these aninit!"

"Ana-nuit," the old man corrected. "The eternal ones."

"You have nothing to fear from them," Micah said. "Not anymore. Tell us, how many are there? And where are they?"

Grandfather buried his face in his hands. "They will come soon. A hundred soldiers, with wagons and weapons. You cannot fight them. The Ana-nuit will punish us all."

After that, he refused to speak any more. Micah gave Socrates a helpless look. The ape shook his head. "I'm afraid we may have done more damage here than we can undo," he said.

At that moment, Loren called out to Socrates. The Tal'mar man had been watching over the body of Anu-Abas. The overseer was stirring, but seemed unable to rise.

"Find some rope," Socrates said to River. "Tie him up, and bring him into the pyramid."

Rapa-nu leapt to his feet. "No!" the old man pleaded. "You must not. Only the Ana-nuit may enter the holy chamber."

"Is that so?" said the ape. "And why is that?"

"It is forbidden."

Socrates snorted. "Why am I not surprised?" He turned to face River. "Bind the overseer and bring him into the pyramid. The rest of you, spread out and keep an eye out for other Ana-nuit. Warn us if any appear. Micah... you come with me."

Micah hurried to walk alongside Socrates as they crossed the lawn to the great pyramid. The slaves gave them a wide berth, and most refused to even look at them.

"They're terrified of us," Micah observed. "They're as frightened of us as they are of the Ana-nuit."

"I'm not surprised," said Socrates. "These people have probably never seen other humans, or any intelligent creatures other than their masters."

"The Ana-nuit," Micah said, stroking his long chin. "Socrates, what's different about them? How did they get... smart?"

"That's what I plan to find out," the ape said.

After a long climb up to the main entrance, approximately two-thirds of the way up the pyramid, the pair reached a broad terrace with gardens planted in rows along either ledge. Additional smaller gardens encompassed the pyramid at each level. Some of these were enclosed by canopies, others open to allow the light inside. Here and there, they saw aqueducts and waterfalls feeding the gardens, flowing down from the top of the pyramid.

Brightly colored engravings decorated the entryway in the shapes of drawings and some indecipherable script. Two statues guarded the entrance on either side. These were made of dark iron, inlaid with gold and silver. The statues' bodies appeared human, but their heads were shaped like lions, and each held a spear in one hand and a scepter in the other.

"Are you sure we should go in there?" said Micah.

"Don't lose your courage now," said Socrates. "These people have lived their entire lives in fear of whatever lies beyond these walls. Let's find out what all the fuss is about."

Cool air washed over them as they passed through the entryway. The inside of the pyramid was relatively dark, lit only by a beam of light shining down through the crystal capstone. Micah sniffed, wrinkling up his nose. "It smells... *clean* in here. Like rain. What is that?"

"I believe it might be ozone." Seeing Micah's perplexed look, Socrates elaborated: "It is an atmospheric gas that accompanies lightning storms. The scientific journals in Sanctuary made reference to it, but I'm afraid I never learned more than that."

"Is it safe to breathe?"

"Has a rainstorm ever killed you?"

"No."

"Then I would assume, at least in minute concentrations, that it is safe."

Micah's eyes had adjusted to the darkened interior, and he turned his head, taking it all in. They stood on a balcony located at approximately the middle of the pyramid. At each corner a set of stairs led down to the first floor, and up to the next balcony overhead.

Rising up from the center of the floor was a huge copper tower. It was perfectly circular and smooth, resting on a base of copper and brass windings. It supported a large metallic orb with mirror-like facets that gleamed under the light of the capstone. A giant disk rotated at low speed under the base, driven by a series of gears and a long driveline that extended through the wall to the mechanism outside.

"What is all this?" Micah said.

Socrates stroked his chin, staring at the device. "I believe we may have discovered the power source for their weapons."

"How does it work?"

"I'm not sure." Socrates hurried over to the nearest staircase and made a quick descent to the first level. Micah hurried after him. At ground level, they approached the base of the machine, standing clear of the driveline and the spinning disk. Socrates examined it while Micah stood back and watched.

"It appears to be some sort of energy concentration device," the ape murmured. "It may be some sort of capacitor, or perhaps an amplification device."

"I don't understand," said Micah. "What does it do?"

Socrates tilted his head to the side as he moved around the base of the machine. "If I'm correct, this base plate creates energy as it spins. It's a strange design, but I'm sure it's a generator of some sort. The windings, the copper tower, the orb at the top... I can't be sure, but I think these somehow propel energy through the atmosphere."

Micah stared at him with a blank look. Socrates paused, looking for a way to explain it that the halfling might understand. Before he could, River and Thane arrived. They were looking down from the balcony with Anu-Abas held captive between them.

"Well then," Socrates said, glancing down at Micah. "Shall we find out what's going on here?"

Chapter 12

Shayla located an unoccupied room in the lower tunnels, and she locked herself inside for the duration of the day. The room was void of any comforts or furnishings, and more than once she had to resist the temptation to steal out into the tunnels in search of food. Thankfully, her sense of self-preservation overcame her more mundane needs and she managed to remain safely hidden for many hours.

There was little to do in that tiny space other than rest, and even that was an uncomfortable endeavor on the cold stone floor. When that wouldn't do anymore, she made an effort to relive the events of the past few weeks in her mind. She wondered if there was anything she might have done to avoid this outcome. She wondered if she had perhaps made a mistake in teaching her secrets to the other women.

This of course, was a fool's quest. Shayla wouldn't have done anything different even if she could have. She had stayed at Dragonwall to help the women there (and perhaps to stay close to a certain tall, dark-haired warrior) and that was exactly what she had done. Unfortunately, her meddling had almost done her in. What good did it do to liberate the women of Dragonwall if it cost Shayla her own life? That was more of a sacrifice than she had intended to make. And the fact that they were willing to betray her... She hadn't seen that coming.

Still, Shayla wouldn't have changed anything. For a short time, she had found *meaning* in her existence. That was something she had been severely lacking since the revolution ended in Astatia. It had been a difficult adjustment for her, coming face to face with the reality that she was the sole surviving heir to a throne that no longer existed and nobody wanted. The people had turned their backs on the monarchy, and in effect, turned their backs on her.

It was liberating, she had tried to tell herself. She was free from any responsibility or obligation to her subjects. They weren't subjects anymore. They were free, and she was free as well. But after a lifetime of preparation, that was a hard reality to accept. It left Shayla with a void inside her, a purpose unfulfilled that she could never satisfy.

Or so she had thought, before Dragonwall. When she'd seen the women there -the bruises, the meek glances- Shayla had once again found purpose. Now, she had to wonder if she had taken things a bit too far.

As the hours passed, Shayla could only guess at what was going on in the mountain around her. She couldn't hear anything -not even the ringing sound of the anvils at the forge- and no one passed her doorway. At one point, thinking it might be time to make her move, Shayla ventured far enough from her hiding place to learn what time it was. Thankfully, she didn't need a clock for that. All she had to do was get a look at the position of the main gear in the chronoforge. The steam-powered machine ran on a precise schedule, performing certain tasks at regular intervals with incredible accuracy. It was about as close to a clock as one could get without actually having one.

As it turned out, it was eight p.m. Not late enough to leave yet, but the smell of food drifting down from the dining hall was excruciating. Shayla forced herself back into the room. She settled down on the floor, the elk-hide cloak wrapped tight about her, and spent another four hours sitting there, trying to ignore the rumbling in her stomach.

At last, Shayla left the room and began making her way up the tunnels toward the exit. She knew she wouldn't be alone. Even this late, there would be a handful of people out in the tunnels: maintenance workers repairing the machines that had been used all day, chamber maids finishing their daily chores and preparing for the next morning, knights and pages coming and going on whatever business knights and pages engaged in late at night. In the darkened tunnels of Dragonwall, these were all easily avoided.

It was the guards at the door who were going to present a problem. On her way there, Shayla searched her mind for ways to expedite her escape. She had heard stories of a secret entrance to the mountain, but had not been able to glean its location. Even after months of aiding and supporting the women of Dragonwall, they still hadn't taken her into their confidence.

She considered other ideas... a distraction, perhaps. A noise down the hall, a fire, anything that might draw the guards away from the keep doors for just a few seconds. But none of her ideas were satisfactory. Even if they succeeded, there remained one major problem yet to confront: what to do *after* she made it out?

She would have to travel, preferably somewhere to the west or north, where there were no dragons. If that was her goal, she wouldn't make it far traveling on foot, wearing nothing but an old elk hide cloak. No, what she needed was a good reliable form of transportation.

Now *that* was a good idea, she thought. And she knew just where to find it...

Shayla made her way to the stables -the large room near the entrance, where the knight's mechanical chargers were housed and maintained- and slipped inside. She found a mechanic there working on one of the horses. He was alone, but she couldn't risk a confrontation. Her nudity was only a minor inconvenience compared to her real problem: a complete lack of weapons. On any other night, Shayla would have had a dozen different choices ready at hand, everything from knives and blades hidden discretely upon her person to a choice of mild tranquilizers and instantly lethal poisons. One man alone at night would hardly have been a hindrance. But that was then, and this was now. Shayla had nothing but her wits.

Shayla moved along the back wall, hidden in the shadows. The mechanic sat on a stool across the room, bathed in the light of a solitary lamp as he hammered and ratcheted his way through the bowels of a crimson red mechanical horse.

Shayla threw her gaze back and forth. She almost immediately found a dozen useful items: hammers, wrenches, saws, rope... any number of means for one person to kill another. But that wasn't her goal. It wasn't Shayla's way to kill an innocent, unarmed man. Despite what the others believed about her, Shayla had a deep belief in the value of human life. Some were more valuable than others, for certain -and some not worth anything at all- but in most cases, life was precious.

Then it occurred to Shayla that she still possessed one of her weapons, and it was perhaps the most powerful she had in her arsenal: beauty. Shayla knew no man could resist her charms. It was not a matter of vanity or boasting, it was a simple fact. Shayla had a refined, elegant beauty about her that was a natural advantage. She also had years of training to supplement that beauty. As a child, Shayla had been trained in every manner of espionage and survival. The soldiers knew they might not always be there to protect her, and she might need the ability to defend herself or to blend in with other people and cultures. One of the most useful skills was one that had always come natural: *flirtation.*

Shayla stepped out of the shadows, boldly crossed the room with the cloak pulled about her, the hood pulled up to conceal her mutated features, her naked feet making tiny sounds against the cold stone floor. The mechanic didn't notice her until she was upon him. If Shayla had wanted to kill him, it would have been all too easy. She giggled and said:

"Hey, handsome."

The mechanic bolted upright, banging his head on the horse's access panel. He stumbled back, tripping over the stool, and went sprawling across the floor in front of her. His crescent wrench clattered across the stones and his breath went out in a loud *oomf!*

"Oh, my!" Shayla gasped. "Are you all right?"

The mechanic shot her a disgusted look and then did a double take. His gaze lingered, sliding up and down her body. Shayla wore the cloak wrapped about her, closed at the front, but her legs were exposed and he saw more than enough to guess how little she wore underneath it. Which was exactly what she had planned.

He was an average-looking man. Average height, average girth, average dark brown hair and matching eyes. Looking the man up and down, Shayla realized there wasn't a single thing about him that *wasn't* average, from the grease stains on his forehead to the hole in the toe of his left boot. But when he glanced into her eyes, Shayla saw his anger melt into helplessness. All at once, he became a stammering, stuttering, love-struck fool:

"I'm... I'm sorry. I didn't see you there...Miss?"

"Shayla," she said softly.

"Yes, yes, of course! I know who you are! Who could forget such a beautiful-" He stopped short, his face flushing with embarrassment. "A proper lady, I mean."

Shayla raised an eyebrow. She stepped closer, gazing down at him. "You think I'm beautiful?" she said with feigned innocence.

He seemed to remember suddenly that he was still on the floor. He swung his legs around, lurching so quickly upright that he bounced in the air before landing on the soles of his boots. Shayla smiled.

"My name's Dom," he said with a slight bow of his head

"I'm sorry, Dom," she said. "I didn't mean to frighten you."

"Not at all, Miss Shayla. Of course not."

"It's just that I couldn't sleep, and I thought how fun it would be to come look at your beautiful horses."

He grinned stupidly. She walked past him, approaching the machine he had been repairing.

"I saw you working on this one," she said. "Did you make them?"

"Oh, no. I just repair 'em."

"I see," she said, looking a little disappointed. "Well, we can't all be perfect."

His face fell. "No, Miss Shayla."

"They are quite complex machines though, aren't they? I suppose working on them must take quite a bit of intelligence."

His face lit up. "Yes, indeed. I've tried to train some of these knights, but they just can't pick up a thing. Heads full of rocks, if you ask me."

Shayla turned to face him. "Dom, do you think maybe... do you think I could ride one?"

"Oh, I don't know if that would be a good idea, being the knight's horses and all. It wouldn't be a-"

Shayla relaxed her grip on the cloak, allowing it to part in front of her. Dom glanced down and his eyes widened as he saw her full nudity exposed in front of him. His faced turned a deep, dark shade of red that was almost purple.

"Just for a minute?" she said teasingly. "Maybe that one over there?" She pointed at the blue one. Dom licked his lips and cleared his throat.

When the two guards standing at the front gate heard the ringing sound of hooves on stone behind them, they didn't pay much attention. The knights of Dragonwall came and went at all hours. The younger guard was telling a crude joke, which was the latest in a string of them going back half of their shift. When he finished, his companion bellowed with laughter.

"The queen would never do that," he said. "Not with you, and certainly not with a dragon!"

As their laughter subsided, they realized that the mechanical horse up the tunnel was galloping at an unusually high speed. That never happened inside the tunnels. It wasn't safe.

As they turned to see what was the matter, Shayla went racing by, cloak flapping in the wind, her glorious nudity on full display. The guards saw her and their eyes went wide. One dropped his spear. They both turned to stare at her as she zoomed past them, through the doors, and went racing down the hill towards Stormwatch. As she vanished into the night, the two men exchanged baffled grins.

Half a second later, Dom appeared. He was red-faced and breathless, dripping with sweat. "Where'd she go?" he demanded. The guards glanced at each other. Their grins faded.

Chapter 13

River released the safety on her revolver and touched the end of the barrel to the overseer's forehead. "How many?" she repeated, her upper lip curling in a snarl. "Tell the truth, or I'll splatter your brains all over this pyramid."

Anu-Abas grinned, his icy blue leather-like skin wrinkling in all the wrong places. The decaying flesh pulled tight around his mouth, and his lips seemed to pucker, exposing the rotten teeth underneath. His vacant eye bulged as if it would burst forth from the socket, and the lenses over his right eye *whirred* as they twisted back and forth.

"Ten thousand men," He said. "Two thousand chariots and twenty-seven hundred riflemen. My people will swarm over you like a horde of locusts. They will cut you down, and when you are dead, they will raise you back to life so they can torture you for a thousand years!"

River lowered the revolver with a sigh. She turned to face Socrates, who had been standing behind her supervising the interrogation. "It's no use. Everything this monster says is a lie."

Socrates stroked his chin thoughtfully. "River, come with me. Thane and Micah, keep an eye on him."

River holstered her weapon and followed Socrates out of the pyramid, into the bright sunshine. She squinted against the light as her eyes adjusted. Socrates turned to the right, strolling into the garden. His footsteps were heavy against the stone walkway, and his gears clicked noisily as he moved.

"The heat's not good for you," River observed. "We should put some fresh grease on your joints."

"I'm fine," he reassured her. "My mechanic has been so zealous about my maintenance that I'll probably outlast the stars." He added that last part with a wink that brought a smile to River's face.

"Not if ten thousand Ana-nuit show up here tomorrow," she said.

"I highly doubt that is going to happen."

They passed under a tall arbor and into a long trellised walkway. The air became cool and aromatic. Grapevines, fruit trees, and scented vines rose along the path, creating a shaded walkway that was almost tunnel-like. They could hear the quiet gurgling sounds of water moving through the aqueducts and waterfalls around them, spilling into ponds and planters along the way.

This, River had learned, was the work of the tall gear-driven structure on the north wall of the pyramid. The device served multiple purposes. It was driven by a high-pressure underground waterline that originated somewhere in the surrounding mountains. The force of the water turned the great gears, which in turn ran the pumps that fed the pyramids, gardens, and the surrounding village. The machine also served a secondary purpose as the driveline to the generator inside the pyramid. The purpose and workings of that device unfortunately remained a mystery.

As the canopy of vines and branches closed in overhead, River inhaled the sweet perfume of the deep blue lilacs that dangled down from the latticework.

"This place is amazing," she said. "I wouldn't mind living here... at least for a while."

"Really?" Socrates said, cocking an eyebrow.

River sighed. "I suppose not. I've never been good at staying in one place. Not since Tinker died, anyway." She gazed through foliage at the villagers down below. "Socrates, I would hate for something bad to happen to these people... especially knowing that it's my fault."

The automaton glanced at her, his neck mechanisms *whirring* as he turned his head. "I believe we share that burden."

"Why do you say that? *I'm* the one who shot the overseer. I started all of this. You told us not to interfere. You've always believed that was best. I broke that rule, and now these people might suffer because of what I did."

Socrates took a deep breath, inflating his massive simian chest, and let out a human-like sigh. It was an automatic process designed to cool his inner workings, but so convincing that even River would have thought he was alive if she didn't know better. "I have always said it is of the utmost importance that we respect the cultures and beliefs of the people we encounter. Do you understand why?"

River shrugged. "I don't know. Respect?"

He turned standing next to her as they looked down on the villagers. "Centuries ago, all humanity shared one culture. Since then they have scattered far and wide. After the cataclysm, they became isolated, independent. They evolved. They rediscovered the secrets of a few simple technologies. Smelting and mining, for example. Steam power. Out of their environment and what little knowledge their ancestors retained, hundreds of unique cultures and civilizations have emerged. It is important that we respect that, and try to protect it."

"I understand that, and I've tried, but-"

"Let me finish." He began walking, and River fell in beside him. "As I was saying, that is how I have always felt, but lately I've been reexamining my beliefs. I understand why you did what you did. And considering your past, I should have seen it coming." He nodded at the slave collar on River's throat as he said this. "To be entirely honest, I'm a little ashamed."

River frowned. "What are you talking about?

"My high ideals have cost us more than once. The child you saved today is a perfect example. I saw what was happening -I was horrified by it- and yet failed to act. I had convinced myself that somehow I would make these creatures see reason. But now, after spending a few hours talking to the overseer, I see that was a mistake. Nothing I could have said would have convinced Anu-Abas to spare that child.

"The Ana-nuit are cruel and violent warlords. They've kept these people enslaved for at least four generations, perhaps even longer. They control every aspect of their lives, and there is no way to defend this. Any culture that perpetuates the enslavement of humans and the abuse of children is not worth saving. They must be destroyed."

River's eyes widened. "Socrates, what are you saying?"

"The Ana-nuit are not humans, River. They are something else. Regardless of whether or not we consider them living -that is really beside the point- they are the worst sort of people imaginable. Whatever their goal, they cannot be allowed to increase their numbers.

We must learn their secrets, and do what we can to stop them."

They paused in front of a small pond to watch the brightly colored fish gliding just beneath the surface of the water. Socrates dipped a finger into the pool, and one of the fish came up to suckle on his finger.

"They're so peaceful," he said. "If only the rest of us could be more like these creatures."

"No thanks," said River. "I'd rather not spend my entire life circling a pond, looking for a way out."

Socrates laughed. "Are you so certain that you don't?"

River glared at him "Have you learned anything else about the Ana-nuit from the villagers?" she said.

"A bit. Most of these people don't speak our language. Those who do are not fluent like their masters. They are kept ignorant. Unless, of course, they are chosen."

"Chosen for what?"

"To become one with the Ana-nuit. To swell their numbers."

"I don't understand. You're saying that they can somehow procreate?"

"Not in the conventional way. You and I both know how these creatures are made. What I don't understand yet is how they retain their human-like intelligence."

"Is the starfall different here? Maybe it's more potent?"

"No, in my studies I've learned that increasing the concentration of starfall does not singularly change the effect on the brains of the dead. It's something else, something the Ana-nuit do to them, most likely related to their technology. It appears that they have concocted an elaborate ritual for just such a purpose."

"A ritual for *murder?*"

"Indeed. According to the grandfather, the Ana-nuit hold a ceremony where they choose certain individuals from among the slaves. They call this an initiation. They bring these people into the pyramid to *convert* them."

"You mean kill them!"

"Of course. The humans know nothing about this. They never get to see the inside of the pyramid, so they don't know what happens in there. They consider it a great honor to be invited inside."

"And then they're murdered? That's sick."

"These slaves are simple people, River. They don't understand how it happens. The Ana-nuit tell them that it's a magical rite."

River stepped away from the fishpond, peering out between the tree trunks at the people working in the streets below. They seemed so far away, so small...

"How can they not understand?" she said. "We've all seen what happens to the dead here."

"They have an ancient tradition of burning the bodies. They've been doing it so long that they don't even remember why it began. They've never seen what happens when a human dies and the starfall reactivates his motor cortex."

"Incredible," River said. "All this time, the Ana-nuit have been keeping them ignorant, and then taking advantage of that ignorance to control them. They don't even understand the most basic things about themselves." She turned to face him. "Why are the Ana-nuit different? How can the way they are murdered affect what they become after they die?"

"It's impossible to say. Unfortunately, we won't glean any information from the overseer. Not directly, anyway."

She stared at him. "What do you mean by that?"

Socrates grinned. "The Ana-nuit may not be human, but they're close enough. They give away more than they mean to. The way they speak, the things they choose to reveal, even their body movements betray them."

"In what way?"

"Anu-Abas claims thousands of men will come here soon, yet we can clearly see that the resources of this village are already stretched. It could only support a few hundred at most, and not for long. It wouldn't make sense for such a large number to come here. If there were hundreds or thousands- of these creatures nearby, only a fraction of that number would be necessary to retrieve the harvest."

"So you think Grandfather was correct? How can you be so sure?"

"Because the overseer isn't a very good liar. And Grandfather has no reason to lie. It is still a large number, of course, but it gives me hope." He paused and gave her a sideways glance. "Have you noticed what the slaves have been harvesting?"

"Of course. They bring those red grapes by the cart and barrelful. What about them?"

"Those grapes are the harvest the old man referred to. The Ana-nuit will be coming to collect the grapes, or perhaps just the juice."

River frowned. "But why? What use would the undead have for grape juice?"

The ape's smile widened. "That's the question, isn't it? I'm going to run some tests to confirm my suspicions, but I believe there is something very special about these wild jungle grapes."

"Do you think the juice keeps them alive? That it has starfall in it?"

"Perhaps. I won't know more until I conduct my tests, and I'd rather not speculate."

They fell silent for a few seconds. River considered what she had learned, and a strange question popped into her head. "Socrates, do you think the Ana-nuit have souls?"

Socrates stared at her. "Souls?"

"Yes, you know... the life force, the spark. The thing that makes us what we are."

"I'm vaguely familiar with the concept," he said. "I've never studied it in depth, I'm afraid."

"I'm sorry, Socrates. I didn't mean to hurt your feelings. I wasn't thinking..."

"I am not offended. After all, who's to say I don't have a soul?"

River grinned. "I never thought about that."

"Or, perhaps none of us have souls. I suppose we shall find out, someday."

River sighed. "So what do we do now? We can't leave these people to defend themselves."

"I agree, especially since their troubles are our own doing."

"But what can we do? Our crew is less than thirty people now, and some aren't good fighters."

"True, but what if we had help?" Socrates said, gesturing at the city below.

"These people haven't ever used weapons, Socrates. They don't even *own any*. And they're terrified of their masters."

"Then we shall have to find a way to use that to our advantage."

River bit her lip. "We're all going to die here, aren't we?"

Socrates grinned. He patted her on the shoulder and said, "Don't be such a pessimist. Maybe the Ana-nuit will make you immortal."

River didn't see the humor.

At that moment, they heard a shout in the distance. "Stop him! Someone stop him!"

River locked eyes with Socrates. "That was Micah!" she said.

"Anu-Abas," the ape growled. They both broke into a run.

River raced ahead of Socrates, until the mechanical primate lowered himself into a crouch and swung his legs forward through his arms. The momentum of this movement carried his weight into the air, allowing Socrates to leap several yards in one bound. He landed, next to her, catching himself on both hands, and repeated the movement. His legs and torso swung forward and he went somersaulting through the air ahead of her. As the simian landed, the springs in his arms made loud *whoosht-clack!* sounds, and the palms of his hands slapped down on the paving stones with the dulled *klang* of flesh-covered metal. In three leaps, he soared past her and reached the corner.

Socrates disappeared around the edge of the pyramid. River flew around the corner a moment later, just in time to see Socrates barreling down the stairs after Anu-Abas. At the top of the stairs, Micah stood watching in disbelief. Thane appeared behind him, holding a bloody kerchief to his nose.

As Socrates bore down on Anu-Abas, it became clear that the undead creature would not escape. To their surprise, he swung to the left and leapt into the air. In an instant, he vanished over the ledge. Half a second behind him, Socrates reached edge of the stairs and froze, gazing down at the field below. River raced down to join him. She arrived a moment later with her revolver in hand, panting as she struggled to catch her breath.

On the grass below, she saw the crumpled shape of the overseer's body. The fall had been too much for his fragile bones; the landing had crushed him instantly. The overseer must have known it would happen, she realized. No one could have survived a drop like that, especially not the overseer with his frail rotting shell of a body. River drew her gaze back to Socrates.

"He committed suicide?" she said. "Why would he do that?"

Socrates frowned, and a jet of steam exhausted out of the chimney behind his ear. His midnight blue fur glistened in the afternoon light. "What are life and death to a creature like that?" he said. "Perhaps Anu-Abas feared death less than the consequences of his failure. Come; help me to dispose of the body. We have plans to make…"

Chapter 14

Erin led Kale and Gavin in a slow but steady climb along the cliff trail. They traveled only by starlight, in near complete silence, never speaking except for occasional whispers and hand signals when necessary. The only real noise they made were the *clinking* sounds of their armor and the crunch of gravel under their boots. Traveling under such conditions was slow and dangerous, but all three had agreed that it was better to risk a fall than to light a torch and be set upon by a horde of the undead.

The trail eventually crested a ridge, and the path split into three forks. One led to the left, down into the volcanic plains of the Firelands, or Ashago, as it was named on the maps. The other continued straight ahead along the ridge, and the third went to the right, back down into the forest. Erin informed the knights that they would be going to the left.

"The ghouls patrol this route," she said in a hushed voice as they started down the path. "Keep your weapons in hand, and be ready for anything."

They proceeded after her, but soon ended up walking abreast as the trail broadened into a smooth slope. They lost sight of the forest behind them. Ahead stretched a bleak and desolate wasteland, void of any signs of life other than the distant glow of fires around the enemy encampments. There were no trees, no plants, not even a sturdy sage growing in that forsaken place.

The looming black clouds blocked out any starlight, but reflected a dull red glow from the volcanoes that was enough to keep the travelers from stumbling as they made their way down the slope.

As they made their descent, their eyes adjusted until they were gradually able to see the irregular shapes rising up from the scorched earth in the distance. It wasn't long until Sir Gavin began to perceive the true reason for Kale's anxiety. The elder knight's eyes widened as he realized that they were looking across an entire army of the clockwork ghouls.

The creatures were barely visible against the dark ground, except in those moments when they passed near a lava flow, or before the flames of a bonfire. Only then did the knight realize how many there were -at least a hundred thousand, and those were only the visible ones. How many more might there be?

And those tall, dark towers were not landforms, he realized, or even buildings: They were *machines*. As if that weren't enough, he soon heard the distant thumping of a gyroplane's propeller cutting across the sky.

"There," Kale whispered, pointing at a dark spot among the clouds. Gavin raised his gaze and saw the machine moving across the horizon. Nearby, he saw a cluster of airships drifting in the fiery haze of smoke and clouds. Gavin's mind swam with the implications. These undead creatures -these ghouls- had built an army. They had airships and war machines, and there could only be one purpose for such things: They were planning an invasion!

Kale jerked his head to the side, motioning for the others to keep moving. They proceeded along the path in silence. The slope steepened just before it reached the plains. Ahead, massive boulders rose up from the shadows. They were scattered across the land like marbles that rose fifteen or twenty feet in height, some even more, and they lay in piles here and there that resembled the ruins of some ancient civilization.

Erin waved a warning signal. She dropped to a crouch and moved forward with her bow drawn and an arrow nocked. Kale heard voices in the distance and saw the dull glow of a fire reflected on the stones. He drew one of his swords, lowered himself to a crouch, and hurried after her. Gavin followed suit, taking up the rear.

They followed Erin to a circle of stones and moved into position behind one of the larger ones. The voices were louder now, though it was impossible to understand the creatures' guttural speech. It seemed the undead had a language all their own. Erin, positioned at the outside, motioned for Kale to look around her. He leaned out, stretching just far enough to see the path ahead.

Kale saw a dozen ghouls gathered around a large bonfire about twenty yards away. On the far side of the flames, he recognized Sir Flynn. The young knight had been crucified to the base of a twisted old juniper. Flynn's armor had been stripped, his arms spread wide, palms facing out, heavy iron spikes hammered through his wrists, deep into the tree. Blood ran down his bare arms and streamed down his chest. His face was bruised and bloody, barely recognizable from the swellling.

One of the ghouls shouted something, and when Flynn didn't answer, the creature whipped him across the chest with a leather strap. The knight let out an involuntary scream, and his body shuddered with pain.

Fresh rivulets of blood ran down his torso. All around, the ghouls started laughing. One came forward, drawing a dagger, and drove it deep into his thigh. Kale cringed as he heard the sound of the blade scraping against bone. Flynn screamed.

"Is that Flynn?" Gavin whispered.

Kale nodded. "They're interrogating him," he said in a low voice.

The old knight wrinkled up his forehead. "For what?"

"For everything," Erin whispered with a dark look. "They want to know everything about us. Where our cities are, how well they are defended... how big our army is. They did this in Ravenwood as well."

In the distance, Flynn cried out again. Kale drew his sword, and took a step away from the boulder.

"No!" Erin hissed, catching him by the arm. "There are too many. They would kill us all."

"I've got to do something," Kale said. "The two of you get out of here. Wait for me at the chargers."

"Don't be ridiculous," said Erin. "You'll only get yourself killed. Let me handle this."

She nocked an arrow to her bowstring and stepped around him. Kale frowned. "What are you doing? You only have four arrows against a dozen of them!"

She shot him a meaningful glance. Kale's eyes widened as he realized what she meant to do. He put a hand on her arm.

"Erin, don't. There must be another way."

"There is no other way," she said. "We can't help Flynn now, and he won't live long anyway. It's better if we make it fast. He doesn't deserve a death like this."

"They've almost killed him already," Gavin said. "The boy's going to bleed to death soon enough."

"Then it's time to end it," Erin said. She moved to step around Kale, but the tall warrior reached down and closed his hand around the bow.

"Let me do it," he said under his breath. "It's my responsibility."

Erin nodded. She released her grip, and Kale took the bow. He stepped up to the edge of the boulder, drew back the string, and sighted down the shaft of the arrow. His gut churned and a cold sweat broke out on his brow.

Kale had killed before, Vangars, mostly. A few undead. He had no problem taking the life of an evil creature like that. But this was... this was different. Flynn had been no great friend to Kale, but he was still an ally. More than that, he was barely more than a child. He hardly seemed old enough to carry a sword, much less carry one into battle. It wasn't right, ending the boy's life like this-

The ghouls lashed out with the whip again, and the young knight screamed. The leather strap cut through his flesh and deep into his muscles. All around him, the ghouls laughed and taunted, throwing rocks and sticks at him, mocking him in loud voices:

"Not so pretty now, are you mortal?" one of them said in the common tongue, in a voice loud enough to hear.

"He's uglier than you!" another laughed.

Kale fought back the bile rising in his throat. He glanced at his companions and whispered in a low grunt, "Be ready."

He took a deep breath and held it. Then, with the practiced perfection of an expert warrior, he released the string. The bowstring sang as the missile sped across the clearing, *whooshing* through the flames. It *thudded* deep into Flynn's chest and the young knight gave out one last whimper. His head lolled, and his body went limp.

There was a moment of silence and then a chorus of shouts as his captors struggled to comprehend what they had just witnessed. Those who didn't see what had happened pushed closer, trying to get a view of their murdered captive. The others, eager to break free of the circle and locate their attackers, found themselves surrounded. They began fighting, pushing back at their companions, even punching them when they failed to move.

Kale handed Erin her bow and the group broke into a run. The three scrambled up the slope as the uproar exploded behind them. There was no more need for silence. It was an open sprint, and this time, they knew the path.

As the companions flew up the hillside, the confused voices of the ghouls grew distant. Kale knew that by the time the creatures organized themselves to launch a counterstrike, it would be too late. They reached the mountain ridge shortly, and paused there long enough to take a few deep breaths and determine if they were being followed. Kale was panting from the climb, his ribs still aching from his earlier battles. Every breath sent jolts of pain coursing through his body. He wanted more than anything to stop, but knew he couldn't.

"I don't hear any voices," Gavin said between breaths. "That could be good news, or bad."

"Better not to find out," Kale said, turning east along the ridge. "Let's get to the horses. Then we can rest."

Their earlier climb up the mountain path had taken an hour. Going back down, it took only half that. Despite being sore and tired, they knew the path now, and the lack of light wasn't as much of a hindrance as it had been before. In fact, in comparison to the dull red haze of the Firelands, the clear starry sky was relatively bright. Kale found himself noting landmarks along the path -an outcropping jutting out overhead, a juniper trunk stretching out of the cliff wall below- and was surprised that he hadn't seen them previously.

A short while later, they arrived at the site of the original battle. They hurried past the corpses littering the area, and quickly covered the last few miles to the horses. They arrived exhausted and dripping with sweat. Kale's breath came in short, painful gasps as he did all he could to pacify his lungs without expanding his rib cage. He climbed into the saddle and offered a hand to Erin.

"Ride with me," he said.

She took his hand and wordlessly swung up behind him. In a flash, they were off.

The trio galloped through Ravenwood just before dawn, and made it out of the woods in time to see the morning sun cresting Dragonwall to the northeast. The ground was slick and shiny with morning dew, and the knights slowed their mounts to a trot as they navigated their way across the ancient lava flows.

As they rode, two knights broke through the tree line to the north and came galloping towards them. Gavin pointed them out, and Kale adjusted his course to meet them. As they drew near, he recognized Sir Bane and Sir Lannis. The latter, astride his green charger and wearing matching black and green armor, pulled up first. He lifted his visor as his mount came to a halt.

"Sir Kale," he said. "I didn't recognize you from a distance. I thought you might be the woman."

Kale frowned. "What woman?"

Sir Bane joined them, halting his gray steed next to Lannis. "The woman from the train," he said. "Shayla. She escaped last night. Stole one of the chargers."

"Escaped?" Kale said. "Escaped from what? When did she become a prisoner? What the devils has been going on?"

The two knights exchanged a glance. "Much has happened since you left," Lannis said.

"I've only been gone one day! Where did she go?"

"We lost her in the woods, west of here. Found the charger half-buried in the river."

"What about Shayla?"

Lannis shrugged. "Washed downriver, perhaps. We searched the far bank, but found no footprints."

"Not that we could be sure," said Sir Bane. "A herd of elk passed through the area this morning. A *bonecrusher* could have driven through there and we'd never know."

Kale glanced over his shoulder at the forest. Gavin leaned close and lowered his voice: "Forget it, boy," he said. "You'll never find her, and you have more important things to attend to."

"Shayla is my friend," Kale said. "She might be in danger."

"Aye, but you are the queen's First Knight, and commander of the militia. Your friend will be fine. I'll send scouts after her the moment we get back."

Kale reluctantly agreed. Gavin was right: he had no choice. As much as he cared about Shayla, Kale had greater responsibilities. For the moment, all he could do was trust her not to do anything stupid. She was smart enough to survive on her own. In fact, Shayla was better trained to do so than most of his knights. Somehow, that didn't ease his worries. What was she doing out there alone? Why had she stolen a charger? He had too many questions to make any sense of it all.

The five of them traveled together for the rest of the ride. Within the hour, they reached Dragonwall. Gavin and the other knights rode into the tunnels to return their mounts for maintenance, but Kale paused to inquire at the front gates about Bathus. The guards there informed him that the knight was in surgery.

Kale did not take that as good news. Surgery was always a last act of desperation. The human body wasn't designed to be cut open; to be poked and prodded and then sewn back together like a rag doll. The practice always resulted in infection, and this wasn't the sort of infection one could simply ignore. Sometimes, it even meant reopening the wound or worse yet, amputating a limb.

But surgery usually just meant death. In Kale's opinion, it was better just to die rather than suffer through a surgery like that for nothing. He felt a pang of regret. Bathus had been a good knight.

"The queen has been awaiting your return," one of the guards informed him. "She requires your presence immediately."

Kale nodded. He helped Erin slide off the charger, and dismounted after her. "You might as well come with me," he said. "You know as much about what's going on as I do."

He handed off the care of his mount to the guard, and then led the way up the tunnel to the main walkway. Erin caught her breath as they entered the mountain. A worker in a giant spring-powered exoskeleton went walking by, and she froze, staring. At the same time, a small self-guided handcart went zipping around his feet and down the slope. It locked up its brakes a few yards down the road, metal wheels screeching as it skidded sideways, and then tore off into one of the tunnels.

"You haven't been here before," Kale said. Erin shook her head and stared at him with wide eyes. "You'll get used to it," he said with a laugh.

Kale put two fingers to his lips and let out a shrill whistle. He held out his hand, waving down a spring-powered wagon that was passing by. The driver, a heavyset man with a long red beard, slowed the wagon enough for them to climb aboard.

The driver looked Erin up and down as she climbed into the seat next to Kale, but didn't say a word. He released the brakes, and they took off with a shuddering jolt. He didn't ask where they were going, but he seemed to know anyway. He powered up the accelerator until they were rolling up the hill at thirty miles per hour. Erin latched onto the safety rail with both hands as pedestrians and workers jumped out of their path. The driver swerved around another vehicle, right up to the handrail at the edge of the road. Erin's stomach did flip-flops as she looked over the edge and saw a three-hundred-foot drop straight into a lake of molten lava.

They pulled back into the middle of the road just as they reached the upper level. The driver locked up the brakes, and they came to a sudden, screeching stop.

Erin jumped out, landing ungracefully on the cobblestones. She stood upright, her bow twisting awkwardly around her. Kale appeared next to her and clapped a hand down on her shoulder.

"That wasn't so bad, was it?"

Erin glared at him as she fussed with her bow, trying to get it unraveled from the quiver and straightened across her back.

"Well, it's not for everyone," Kale said, chuckling. "You probably wouldn't like the other way, either."

He didn't expand on that comment, but instead started walking across the road. Erin hurried after him. At the far side, the couple entered a dimly lit hallway decorated with tapestries, rugs, and wooden furnishings.

"Incredible!" Erin said, staring at one of the tapestries. It portrayed an image of a king and several knights fighting a big black dragon.

"You like it?" Kale said.

"It's all so... so princely. I always wondered what royalty lived like, but I never imagined it could be like this."

Kale raised an eyebrow. "This is just a hallway, kid. Wait 'till you see the queen's chamber."

They proceeded down the hall, and shortly came to a tall wooden door. Kale lifted the knocker, gave it three loud raps, and then went ahead and opened the door. Queen Aileen appeared before them. When she saw Kale, she rushed forward to throw her arms around him.

"Thank the spirits, you're alive!"

Kale returned her embrace and then pulled away. "Aileen, what's going on? What happened to Shayla?"

The queen pressed her lips together. She glanced at Erin and then back at Kale. "Erin can be trusted," Kale said. "She saved my life last night."

The queen sighed. "We have much to talk about..."

Aileen asked one of her servants to prepare tea, and then led the couple through the main room and out onto the veranda. Erin followed haltingly along, pausing to admire the ceramic statues, the gilded birdcage and the massive stone fireplace... she soon found herself standing alone in the middle of the room. Kale and the queen had proceeded on without her.

"Imbecile," Erin said under her breath. *"You're acting like a witless child!"* She straightened her shoulders, tossed her hair, and went marching out to join them.

"...and the next thing anyone knew, she was gone," the queen was saying. They had settled onto cushioned wrought-iron chairs beside a beautiful matching table. Behind the queen, Erin saw the entire land stretching out before her. She could see west and south all the way to the mountains, and to the north, the infinite plains stretching to the horizon.

"And you have no clue what happened to her?" Kale was saying.

"Only that the guards say she was nude."

Kale's eyes widened. "What?"

"Yes, and apparently she had bruises -or what appeared to be bruises- all over her body, and blood on her face, as if she had been fighting."

The warrior's knuckles made cracking sounds as he squeezed his hands into fists. Aileen reached out, putting a gentle hand on his arm.

"I know what you're thinking," she said. "Someone did something to her... something terrible. And I know what you want to do, but I'm begging you not to do it."

Kale locked eyes with the queen. "Someone *beat her*," he said in a growling voice. "And probably raped her, too. I saw your own husband throw a man into the volcano for less!"

"I'm aware of that, and normally I wouldn't interfere. Unfortunately, my grasp on the crown is tenuous enough already. If the people think even for a second that I've lost control of my command, it will be over. They will exile me, or worse."

She leaned closer, lowering her voice as she gazed into his burning blue eyes. "I'm only asking you to be patient," she said. "For just a little while."

Kale closed his eyes and leaned back in the chair, putting a hand to his forehead. "Fine," he said. "I won't act, for now. But I will find out who did this. You need to understand that."

"Agreed, so long as you swear not to act out until I am ready."

Kale nodded.

"Excellent," said the queen. "Now... tell me about what you saw in the Firelands."

Kale's face darkened. He glanced at Erin, and motioned for her to join them at the table. As she settled into one of the chairs, a dark cloud seemed to pass over the group. Kale began to speak in a low voice:

"We need more good fighting men in the militia and more weapons... Where is the *bonecrusher?*"

Chapter 15

Shayla first became aware of the scent of damp musty earth, of rich soil and moss and green growing things all around her. She heard a bubbling brook somewhere nearby, and the scent of water seemed more potent than she remembered. Her eyes fluttered open. Narrow beams of sunlight filtered down through the treetops to form scattered pools of light in the dark forest. She became aware of the cool air washing over her naked flesh, but felt a comfortable warmth against her back.

Shayla heard a snort, and she bolted upright.

As she leapt to her feet and turned, she found herself staring into the face of a massive bull elk. The creature was white as snow, with a long goatee dangling from its chin and sprawling horns that could easily span a room. Even lying on the ground, the beast could look her straight in the eyes. Shayla took a cautious step back, wary of frightening the creature into attacking her. The elk watched her with a patient, knowing stare, but didn't move.

The cloak lay at her feet, but Shayla's complete nudity was for the moment the least of her concerns. Shayla heard noises in the woods around her. There were others nearby: twenty or thirty scattered throughout the trees. Some were standing, others resting. There were many females, and only a handful of males. None were anywhere near the size of the albino.

As Shayla took stock of her situation, her fears began to evaporate. A sense of curiosity overcame her. This animal, this massive white elk, was unlike anything she had ever seen. The soldiers at Fort Hope had hunted elk from time to time, and she had seen some impressively large animals, but none that could compare to this noble beast. The beard was unusual, too. Perhaps it marked this elk as a different species from those with which she was familiar. And the color! Who had ever heard of a ghost-white elk? It must have been exceptionally rare.

There was something else; something about the way it looked at her, the way it smelled, that she found strangely comforting. The creature's gaze seemed almost paternal... protective. Or was she just imagining it?

The bull gazed at her through half-lidded eyes, absently chewing its cud. Shayla summoned her courage and took a step closer. The elk took almost no notice of her. She reached out, daring to touch one of the massive horns. The velvety surface was soft and warm on her fingertips, offering almost no resistance to her touch. It seemed to pulse with life, the tiny fibers almost like living skin. The bone under the velvet was hard and smooth, like stone under a silk sheet. The sensation sent a thrill up her spine. Nothing, Shayla thought, could be this soft.

An image came into her mind: Shayla saw herself lying on the ground, warm sunlight streaming down, baking her skin. She felt the vaguely dizzy sense of sleeping, or daydreaming, and a complete absence of worries or concerns. But these thoughts were not her own... they were thoughts of someone else, of someone watching her. She frowned, trying to understand the meaning.

Rest, said a voice deep in her mind. It was low and soft, like a whisper at the edges of her consciousness. Her eyes widened. She understood. The elk was trying to tell her something. Telling her to rest, to be calm and wait for something... but for what?

Shayla's stomach rumbled. She understood what the elk wanted her to do, but her body needed sustenance. If she didn't find something to eat, she wouldn't have the energy to go on.

"I'm hungry," she said in a quiet whisper. "I need food."

The elk stared at her, not seeming to understand. Shayla closed her eyes. She tried to picture herself eating a meal. She imagined herself sitting at a dinner table, lifting food to her mouth with a fork. She imagined the aroma washing over her, the taste of spices and seasonings on her tongue. While picturing this image, she tried to reach out in her mind to the elk; to make it understand what she was seeing.

The elk shifted, and Shayla opened her eyes. He rose, turned to the side, and headed into the woods. Shayla watched for a moment, confused as he crossed the stream and moved away from her, deeper into the forest. Light and shadow played across his brilliant hide, branches cracking under his hooves. The ferns rustled as the rest of the herd rose to follow him.

The bull paused a few yards off and looked back at Shayla. She stared for another moment, until the creature made an impatient sighing sound. This spurred her into movement. Shayla hurried after the bull, her naked legs splashing through the stream. She realized with some detachment that she seemed hardly aware of her own nudity. She felt strangely comfortable with it, as if the absence of clothing was a completely normal situation. In fact, she only really became conscious of it at that moment, and forgot it again almost immediately. She exited the far side of the stream and hurried down the path, following the white elk towards some unknown destination.

As she walked, the undergrowth slapped at Shayla's bare legs. The branches, rocks, and pine cones bit into the soles of her feet. She felt something -something she might have once considered painful- but now only seemed like a softness; a weakness of the flesh that would soon harden.

The forest gave way to an orchard, and Shayla found herself walking among perfect rows of tall, thin-trunked trees. The branches stretched out overhead, multiple strains of brightly colored fruit dangling down. Shayla scanned the area for low-hanging fruit that might be within reach, but found none. The closest branches were ten feet high.

Observing her struggle, the bull elk came to her side. It made a snorting sound and bent down, lowering its rack to the ground next to her. Shayla hesitated, and the creature snorted again. It was displaying a certain amount of impatience with her, she realized.

Shayla obediently climbed up into its antlers. As soon as she had settled, the elk raised its head, bringing her within easy reach of the branches. Shayla reached out and plucked an orange-colored, bell-shaped fruit. She put it to her lips, sinking her teeth into the soft flesh. Ripe, sweet juice exploded into her mouth, dribbling over her lips and down her chin. Shayla's stomach rumbled greedily, and she reached for more.

She spent some time eating, until at last the bull sensed her satisfaction and lowered Shayla to the ground. She reclined back on the soft earth, gazing up at the deep blue sky. Her hands and face were sticky and sweet, and the perfume of the fruit seemed to envelop her. This mingled with the scent of the earth and the woods, and of the herd that had moved in to surround her.

Shayla's eyelids drifted shut, and her cares of the world slipped away like the cloak that had once covered her nudity.

Chapter 16

"Ankasen, raise the bow a little higher," River said, stepping closer to the slave boy. "Sight down the arrow." She touched his left arm, raising it to the proper angle. "Good. Now, shoot!"

Unlike most of the slaves, Ankasen was relatively fluent in the common tongue. He was a smart kid. He had learned the language from listening to the speech of the overseers. He was only ten, but strong for his age, and fearless, too. The whip marks on his back attested to this fact. The question was whether River could find a way to imbue that intelligence and courage into the rest of the village.

Everything River and her companions did they met with suspicion. The villagers had no great love for their Ana-nuit overlords, but at the same time the slaves were too set in their ways, and too unsure of themselves to believe things could ever change. As strange as it sounded, they were actually comfortable with things as they were. They had a set of rules to live by, and overlords to manage their lives for them -to punish or reward them as they deemed fit. It wasn't enjoyable, but it was simple. It was something they understood, and therefore need not fear. Rebellion, on the other hand, was terrifying.

Ankasen released the string, and the arrow left the rest with a *whoosh!* As it did, the bowstring slapped his inner forearm. He let out a painful yelp and dropped the bow. The arrow zoomed in a high arc over the target, missing it by several feet, and vanished into the woods beyond. River watched the arrow disappear into the jungle and knew immediately that they would never find it again. She turned to face Ankasen, who lowered his face shamefully.

"It's all right," she said, clapping a hand on his shoulder. "You did very well. Go see the priest about your injury."

River watched the boy sulk away. Of all the slaves, Ankasen had shown the greatest capacity for learning. Only a handful of the others had managed to successfully draw a bow that day, or even hurl a spear. None had come as close to the target as the boy. He had no fear of learning like the others. She couldn't help wondering if the rest were even capable of it.

Socrates had been standing a few yards back, watching her. River sighed as she approached the automaton. A slight grin twisted his simian features into a caricature of a human smile, but otherwise he stood perfectly still. Unnervingly still. Sometimes, when Socrates was deep in thought or concentrating on something, he looked almost like a statue.

"Not going well?" he said.

"That's an understatement. They can't learn this, Socrates. They can't use bows, they can't use spears... I wouldn't even dream of giving one of these people a sword. The closest thing to a weapon they know how to use is a hoe. They'll never survive a real fight."

Socrates stroked the fur on his cheeks, and pinched his chin between his thumb and forefinger. "What about crossbows?" he said.

"Are you kidding? I wouldn't go within fifty yards of one of these people if he had a crossbow. They're a hazard. The only thing *not* in danger is the target!"

Socrates chuckled, and a little puff of steam rose from his chimney. "We may be taking the wrong approach," he said.

"What do you mean?"

"If we can't train these people to fight, then we'll have to find a way to use their passivity to our advantage."

It was River's turn to laugh. "Great plan," she said. "When the horde of undead warriors gets here, we'll just ignore them to death."

Socrates didn't respond. He was stroking his chin, gazing off into the distance. River stared at him.

"You're serious, aren't you?"

"There is an ancient proverb about warfare: A wise warrior will use his enemy's strength against him."

"How can we do that?"

"We must start by understanding the Ana-nuit. What are their strengths? What are their weaknesses?"

"I don't know about weaknesses, but they have the strength of numbers. They also have superior technology."

"Not necessarily superior, just different. Their ability to store energy and transfer it through these scepters is impressive, but it does have drawbacks."

"Such as?"

"It's not a ranged weapon. It is only useful in hand-to-hand combat and only at a distance of a few yards. It would be useless against a rifle, or even a bow."

"Maybe they have a bigger version, like a cannon."

"That is doubtful. I have discussed the Ana-nuit with the slaves in great detail, and they made no mention of any such weapon."

"Fair enough. Even if you're right, they still have a large force of trained fighters. They will be well armed, and they'll have chariots. Maybe even other technologies we haven't seen yet. These people can't fight against that."

"You are correct."

"Then it's impossible to beat them. You've admitted as much."

"I've done no such thing. I agree that they are a superior fighting force, and we stand no chance against them in open battle. You and I know that, and they will know it from the first moment they see us. That is what we will use against them."

"You're not making any sense."

Socrates handed River the scepter he'd been studying. She turned it over in her hands.

"That is a powerful weapon," he said, "but it has inherent weaknesses. It only operates within a hundred yards of the large pyramid."

"So what? If the Ana-nuit come marching in here with fifty men, we won't be able to keep them at a distance."

"That's what I'm counting on," the ape said.

River shook her head. "I'm not following you."

"What do you suppose would happen to that weapon if we ramped up the voltage by say fifty percent?"

"I don't know, maybe it would overheat? Or malfunction?"

"Perhaps," said Socrates. "I think it's a question worth looking into, don't you?"

A wicked smile twisted up the corners of her mouth. "I guess I'd better find out."

"Excellent," said Socrates. He turned and started walking across the lawn, towards the steamwagon parked nearby.

"Wait!" River called after him. "Where are you going?"

"To the train. I have a few tests of my own to run!"

Chapter 17

Thane had been waiting to talk to River. When she didn't show up for supper, the bard decided to track her down on his own. The mechanic wasn't in the village, but Micah said she might still be in the largest pyramid, where she had been working on a project for Socrates. The gentlemanly thing, Thane decided, would be to bring River a plate so she wouldn't go hungry.

This had seemed a simple enough proposition, until the bard actually started *climbing* the pyramid. The structure's stairs were taller than normal stairs, and within the first few yards, Thane began to second-guess his generosity. He was already breathless, and wasn't sure he could even make it to the entrance without spilling the plate, much less get there while the food was still warm.

He wasn't willing to admit defeat yet, though. He removed his cloak, hanging it over his arm, and proceeded on his way.

The bard quickly developed an appreciation for the engineering involved in the massive structure. It was like climbing a mountain, except that this mountain had been carved by human hands, and many of the stones were the size of a house. It was inconceivable that such a structure could have been built with the crude technology he had seen in the village. The only explanation was that the Ana-nuit had designed the structure, and guided the slaves in the building process. Even if that was the case, it was still a remarkable accomplishment. Where had they found stones that size? And how had they been moved? Unfortunately, the villagers had already proven reluctant to discuss their overlords, and even less so their incredible structures.

When he at last reached the entrance at the midway point, Thane turned to face the village and was rewarded with a clear view for miles in every direction. It was truly breathtaking. To the east, he could see moonlight reflected in the sparkling waterfalls where the ocean spilled over the rim of the crater. In the other directions, the treetops formed bulging protuberances that in the dim twilight appeared like dark clouds floating across the earth.

Thane couldn't imagine a more romantic spectacle, and it was disappointing that he didn't have someone to enjoy it with him. Shayla would have appreciated such a view, but unfortunately, she had made her decision. It was time for the bard to accept that and move on. He took a deep breath, inhaling the sweet aroma of lilacs. With a quiet sigh, he entered the pyramid.

It was dark inside, the interior lit only by a handful of torches and the dull glow of the crystal capstone at the apex. Thane blinked, trying to get his eyes adjusted to the darkness. He approached the balcony rail, looking down into the chamber, and saw only machine parts and dark shadows. The copper tower sizzled with electricity. Tiny tendrils of lightning crawled up the skin of the machine to leap into the capstone with a blue flash. This happened every few seconds, and with every release of energy, the glow of the capstone brightened and then gradually began to decrease.

"River?" Thane said, his voice echoing through the dark interior. She didn't answer, so he took the stairway down into the bowels of the pyramid.

It was darker here, so far from the glowing capstone. Thane took a torch from the wall and approached the tower at the center of the room. The disk turned, energizing the copper tower. The noise of machinery and water pumps filled his ears, and the scent of metal and grease washed over him.

Thane heard a noise behind the metallic disk and followed the sound around back. River was there, hidden in the shadows with a long screwdriver in one hand and a lantern in the other. She was in a state of deep concentration, studying the many copper wires, pipes, and conduits that extended out of the machine. She reached up to tap one of the conduits, and then took a few steps to the side as she traced it to its origin.

Thane was not surprised by River's fascination with the machine. She was enamored of all things mechanical, and when she found something like this that she didn't understand, she would study it until she had extracted all its secrets one by one. The bard didn't say anything, but instead stood watching her. River reached up, touching another of the overhead pipes, and Thane couldn't help admiring her figure as she stretched out, exposing her bare midriff.

River was beautiful -far more so than she seemed to know- and to Thane, watching her was like appreciating a work of great art. River had fine, almost platinum blonde hair and light skin. These attributes she had inherited from her mother, who was half Tal'mar, but she also had the dark eyes and sturdy build of her deceased father, and this made her something of an enigma. Thane had never known a woman quite like her: so gorgeous, yet as formidable in a fight as any man. River never ran from a confrontation. Often enough, she started them.

After a few moments, the bard began to feel a bit guilty about his voyeurism. He cleared his throat to get her attention. River, who had been bending over one of the conduits, straightened so fast that she hit her head on part of the framework. The metal made a loud *clanging* noise that reverberated up and down the shaft. Thane winced.

"My apologies. I didn't mean to startle you."

"I didn't hear you come in," River said, rubbing the back of her head.

"I didn't see you at dinner. I thought I would bring you a plate." He held up the food he had brought, and River smiled.

"Oh! What time is it, anyway?"

"Late. Nearly ten."

"Is Socrates back from the train?"

"He's been coming and going. Last I saw, he was inspecting the grape harvest. Turns out the ghouls love those things. They eat the fruit, they turn the juice into wine. There's an entire cellar full of barrels beneath the smaller pyramid."

"I must have been right then," she said absently. "The juice of those grapes must contain starfall."

She tossed her screwdriver into the toolbox, and accepted the tray of food the bard brought for her. River settled down on the edge of the platform and Thane took a seat next to her. He threw his gaze around the room.

"What have you been working on?"

"Good question. I'm trying to amp up the power, but I can hardly understand this system. The flywheel plate is the generator -that part is obvious, you can tell by the magnets- but the rest is like nothing I've ever seen." She craned her head back, following the pipes and circuits with her eyes as they climbed toward the apex. "I've reworked the gears to bring up the RPMs, and I'm doubling the wire gauge. That ought to get things moving in the right direction, but I won't know until I can test it..." Her voice drifted off. She bit off a crust of bread and chewed it absently as she continued studying the machine. Thane cleared his throat.

"River, there's something I've... something I need to tell you."

She pulled her gaze back to meet his. Thane felt a slight swooning, as if the gravity of her being was drawing him in. It seemed she could look right into his soul. River narrowed her eyebrows.

"What is it?"

"I worry about you... you work so hard, and you never take time to rest-"

"I'm fine," she said with a grin. "I'm a big girl. You don't need to worry about me." She went back to her food, and Thane watched her eat in silence.

She is not a delicate eater, the bard realized, watching her wolf down the last of a slice of bread. Even so, she was still somehow beautiful. He couldn't help smiling. Unfortunately, River caught him.

"Is something funny?" she said around her mouthful.

"Do you like the food?"

"I've had better."

"When this is all over, perhaps I could cook for you again."

Their eyes locked. Thane felt the swooning again, and River seemed almost unable to look away. Feeling that it was now or never, Thane leaned close. The bard pressed his lips tight against hers, and closed his eyes.

The world seemed to melt away. He felt the warmth of her mouth against his own, the taste of salt on her lips, the scent of sandalwood rising from her throat. Chills crawled across his skin. His eyelids drifted open, and-

Whomp! Stars flashed through his vision. His skin burned, and his cheek instantly started to swell. River was already on her feet with both hands knotted into fists. She flexed the right one; the one that had just hit him, but Thane reached out and caught her by the wrist.

"Wait! I'm sorry, I didn't mean-"

"I think I know what you didn't mean," River said, jerking away. She went rushing out of the pyramid, leaving Thane sitting next to her half-empty plate. He absently rubbed his swollen cheek. He didn't really feel the pain. It wasn't his cheek that was hurting, it was something else; something he didn't want to admit.

This took the bard by surprise. It may not have been as sudden as River's wallop, but it was at least as shocking. When had he begun to feel this way about her? He had never felt this way when Shayla was around. Why was that? Had her presence comforted him that much? Or, was it that now she was gone, he could understand his real feelings? What were his real feelings?

Thane rose to his feet. He ambled across the floor, towards the stairs, and made the short climb up to the balcony. He seemed suddenly very aware of everything around him: the dusty, ozone-tinged smell of the air inside the pyramid, the rustle of his clothing, the sound of his boot heels on the hard stone, the noise echoing all around...

He walked through the threshold, out onto the dais. The world seemed to open up before him. Stars twinkled in a midnight blue sky, their silver light falling down to dance across the treetops. The moon hung suspended over the jungle like a pendant. Here and there, torches flickered among the streets in the village. The air was thick with the scent of lilacs and incense and fermenting grape juice.

Thane heard a sound behind him and swung his head around, taking an instinctive step back. He relaxed as he saw River leaning against the pillar at the entrance. He hadn't noticed her there in the darkness. Their eyes met, and he felt that painful gnawing at his insides once again. Almost worse than her reaction was his own feeling of guilt. What had he done to their friendship? What if she couldn't forgive him?

River's eyes glistened in the moonlight, her hair shimmering. He waited for her to say something, but she only stared. A moment passed, and his sense of discomfort grew.

"River, I'm sorry-" he started to say, but the moment he began to speak, she sprang upon him. River crashed into him so hard that she drove the bard a step back. His arms flew out to the sides, unbalanced, half expecting another punch to the jaw. Instead, River put her hands to his face and drew it down to meet her own. Their lips met, her hot sweet breath gushing into his mouth, her body soft but surprisingly powerful against his own.

Thane forgot what he was about to say, forgot what he had been thinking, forgot everything that had just happened. He pulled her close against him, squeezing her tight as if in fear she might escape. The stars seemed to swirl around them, and the sweet perfume of the night air settled over them like a blanket.

Chapter 18

The next morning, River woke to the sound of distant voices and the quiet hum of the pyramid's generator. She became conscious of the cold stone floor beneath her, the warm velvet cloak spread over her like a blanket, and the golden light streaming in through the entrance. Her clothes were rumpled and uncomfortable from sleeping in them, and her back ached from sleeping on the stone floor. She blinked, for a moment not quite sure where she was. Then Thane stirred next to her, and it all came back.

River propped herself up, turning so she could face him. The bard's eyes fluttered open. He gazed up at her through his thick blond bangs, and a warm smile came to his lips.

"Morning," he said.

"Hush!" River whispered, tossing the cloak aside. She pushed to her feet and hurried over to the entrance, where she stood at the corner, partially concealed in shadow, and gazed down at the village. Behind her, Thane crawled to his feet, slid on his boots, and walked over to join her.

"What's going on?" the bard said.

River's eyes were wide, her body tense. The rivets on the slave choker around her throat gleamed in the morning light. She turned her head to lock eyes with him. "They're back. The Ana-nuit have returned."

"They weren't supposed to be here yet," the bard said. "The villagers said we had time-"

River stepped back into the shadows, facing Thane. "Apparently, they were wrong."

"What are we going to do?"

"Nothing. We're trapped in here."

Thane licked his lips. "What if they come in here?" River didn't answer, but instead turned her attention back to the field. Thane leaned out, gazing over the top of her head. On the field below, he saw a large gathering of undead soldiers. His eyes widened, and he lowered his voice: "There must be a hundred and fifty of them! That's half again as many as we were expecting."

River didn't answer, but her expression was grim. The ghoul who appeared to be the commander was at the front of the group, standing on a chariot. River's eyebrows narrowed as she studied the charioteer. He was tall. It was difficult to judge his height from that distance, but comparing him to the others -and to Socrates, who stood at the base of the pyramid- the commander appeared to be at least eight feet tall.

His uniform consisted of a long-tailed coat with no sleeves, and a top hat. Long white hair fell down over his shoulders. His left arm was a mechanical framework that made *clicking* sounds as he moved, and his hand was a mechanically operated gauntlet. The entire framework was attached to his shoulder by thick bolts that went right through the bone. He wore an eyepiece similar to the one Anu-Abas had worn, except that this one wasn't permanently attached. Instead, it was secured by a leather strap. Altogether, his appearance was that of a giant half-machine, half-corpse, and it sent a chill down River's spine.

The other soldiers lined up behind him, some on foot, others riding vehicles that looked suspiciously like steamwagons. The ghouls wore minimal armor, mostly patchwork pieces of metal plate, in some cases integrated into the framework of their enhanced decaying bodies. Tiny pistons raised fleshless arms. Coil springs and actuators supported damaged and jointless legs. Armatures with magnifying lenses were attached to their goggles, or screwed directly to the exposed bone around their eye sockets. One ghoul had sword blades instead of forearms, and another had a mace swinging from his left elbow by a chain.

"I am Sergeant Ranash," the white-haired charioteer shouted, his voice echoing through the village as he glared down at Socrates. "Who are you and what are you doing in my city?"

"My name is Socrates. I am a traveler and philosopher. I came here to study these villagers -the Anukhim, as you call them."

Ranash threw a glance around the village. "Where are my overseers?"

Socrates didn't say anything. Sergeant Ranash raised a scepter and pointed it at him. Socrates took a step forward and lowered his head deferentially.

"Forgive me," the ape said in a humble voice. "I'm afraid I accidentally killed them. When I saw your people torturing these slaves, I thought they were monsters."

The sergeant threw his head back, roaring with laughter. "Monsters! I only see one monster here." He stepped off the chariot and approached Socrates. He loomed over the ape, slowly circling around him, the long tails of his coat swishing as he moved. His mechanical hand opened and closed with an unnerving ratchet-like noise. "What did you do with their bodies?"

"I hid them in the jungle," Socrates said. "When I realized what I had done, I hoped to escape your wrath."

"You did this alone?"

Socrates nodded.

"What manner of creature are you? Are you man, or beast?"

Socrates twisted his head slightly as he looked up into the sergeant's face. The ape seemed strangely small next to the ghoul. "I am an autonomous machine. My creator was a toymaker in the great city of Sanctuary."

"A machine?" Ranash said, twisting up his grisly features. He leaned closer, staring into the ape's face. His eyepiece whirled, making tiny *click-clicking* sounds. "You look familiar to me. You look like the creatures that I hunted in the jungle as a child."

This statement took the ape by surprise. His eyebrows went up, and he locked gazes with the sergeant. "You remember being a child?"

Ranash sneered. "Yes, I was Anu-khim, once. A slave, like these people. I was born of woman, before I was reborn as a god. Surely the villagers have explained this to you?"

"They have spoken very little to me," Socrates said. "They fear me."

Ranash seemed to accept this answer. He turned to face the soldiers standing in line behind him. "Take this machine into custody. I wish to study him further. *Aku-habas, renori de kobla-ho. Desi-sada.*"

Two soldiers came forward to take Socrates by the arms. The moment they laid hands on him, there was a shout from one of the nearby buildings, and the crew of the Iron Horse came racing out with their weapons drawn. They were armed with muskets, scatterguns, and bows. The Ana-nuit soldiers raised their weapons, but Ranash held his hand in the air.

"Hold fire!" he commanded. The soldier standing next to him repeated this order, bellowing it out at the top of his lungs. Ranash glanced over his shoulder at Socrates, raising an eyebrow.

Socrates gave him an apologetic smile. "I hoped it wouldn't come to this."

"I see," said Ranash. "What a mystery you are: a machine that looks like a beast and lies like a human. Your creator must have had a sense of humor."

The ape's smile faded and he took a step forward, but the soldiers tightened their grip on him. "Manatho," one of them said in a snarling voice, and pressed his weapon to the automaton's head. The interpretation was a mystery, but the meaning was clear enough.

For a few seconds the two groups faced off, no one speaking or moving. There was a rustling noise as Micah stepped out from among them and approached the sergeant. Micah was the only crewmember without a weapon, but this didn't seem to concern him as he walked past the guards and up to Ranash. The halfling tilted his head back, his long chin jutting out as he stared up at the skeletal giant.

"Release Socrates," he said. "And evacuate this village. You have five minutes to clear out, or we will kill all of you."

The soldiers glanced back and forth at each other. They broke out in hysterical laughter. Even Ranash couldn't help grinning.

"You are a brave little half-man," he said, staring down at Micah. "What a strange creature you are... the size of a child, but... you are a man, aren't you? Your features don't seem human, though..." He lifted his gaze, looking over the rest of the group. His gaze lingered when he saw the Tal'mar.

"Such a strange group," he said. "So many human-like creatures, and yet *not* human. It would be a shame to kill all of you. I have a feeling you have much useful information..."

Sergeant Ranash took a moment to consult with his second in command. The two creatures conversed in hushed tones for a few seconds, and then Ranash raised his mechanical arm high in the air. "Spare the little one," he said. "Kill the rest." His clockwork hand made *clicking* noises as he closed it into a fist. The soldier behind him shouted: "Open fire!"

The crew of the Iron Horse began firing their weapons. Thunderous explosions of gunfire shattered the still. Bullets, arrows, and scattergun pellets struck the Ana-nuit. It seemed they had the upper hand, until they realized the bullets were passing through the soldiers' bodies or bouncing off their mechanical enhancements harmlessly. The arrows *thudded* into decaying flesh, but didn't even phase the clockwork monsters.

The ghouls immediately returned fire. They raised their weapons, targeted the crew, and squeezed the handles. The air *crackled* with lightning. There was a loud buzzing noise and, strangely, electric shocks burst like fireworks in the air all around them. Cries of shock and dismay went up among the ranks as invisible waves of energy rolled through the formation. Clockwork soldiers dropped to the ground, convulsing.

A rogue energy wave blasted the sergeant. It tossed him unceremoniously through the air, and at the same time struck Socrates and Micah, hurling them backwards across the lawn. The chariot flipped over on its side and began to leak a strange, sulfur-smelling liquid. The instant the liquid made contact with wood, thick smoke went churning up, and it burst into flames.

The soldiers back in the ranks did not immediately perceive what had happened to their comrades. They rushed forward to protect them, raising their energy weapons to target the crew. They released a second volley, unwittingly unleashing new torrents of wild energy.

This second barrage was so powerful that several weapons exploded in their users' hands. The ghoul soldiers screamed as their bodies disintegrated. Arcs of electricity went dancing across the field, tendrils forking this way and that, striking out like serpents. The clockwork soldiers fell, shaking with convulsions, the mechanical frameworks on their bodies arcing with electricity. Arms and legs flailed uncontrollably. Jaws snapped open and shut until the ghouls' teeth shattered, and their bones broke into pieces. Joints and brass body parts melted, leaving the ghouls lying helpless in puddles of molten metal.

Some struggled to regain their footing as their bodies lurched and hammered uncontrollably. Others went still, never to move again. The entire spectacle only lasted for about a minute, and it ended quite suddenly with an eerie calm. No one had escaped. The entire battalion had been rendered immobile, unconscious, or dead. The crew of the Iron Horse lay scattered in their path, moaning, limbs still convulsing as the discharge faded.

Sensing her opportunity, River broke into a sprint. Thane reached out to stop her, but she was already gone. With a frustrated shake of his head, the bard took off after her. River drew her revolver as she flew down the stairs. At the base of the pyramid, she leapt onto the field and ran through the bodies of the fallen until she found Socrates in their midst. She dropped to her knees at his side.

River called out his name, shaking his shoulders. "Socrates, wake up!" She slapped his furry cheeks and shook him. "Wake up, we need you now!"

The machine didn't move.

"Is he dead?" Thane said, hovering at her side.

"I don't know... the discharge may have overloaded his circuits."

"Will he be okay?"

River didn't say anything, but gave him a dark look. Thane noticed Micah lying on the grass a few yards away, and he hurried over to the halfling. Micah stirred as Thane touched him.

"What happened?" Micah said.

Thane helped Micah up to a sitting position and they both gave River a questioning look. She sighed.

"I boosted the generator's amplification signal, and reversed the polarity," she said. "Socrates thought it would overload their weapons."

"It overloaded more than that," Micah said wryly.

"I didn't expect the Ana-nuit to keep using their weapons. They were supposed to stop when they saw they weren't working..."

"You underestimated their stupidity," said Micah.

"Be careful, little one," said a low voice.

They jerked their heads around to see Sergeant Ranash looming behind them. He had retrieved a fallen scattergun, and held it trained on them. His top hat was gone, revealing the gleaming bleached white cap of his skull. The silvery-white hair that fell around his shoulders grew from thin strips of flesh along the sides of his head.

Behind the sergeant, a few of the Ana-nuit were crawling back to their feet. River reached for her revolver, but Ranash took a step closer and pointed the barrel of his weapon at Micah's head. His eyepiece made *whirling* noises as it adjusted focus and a grim smile came to his lips.

"Drop your weapon," he said to River, the skin on face pulling into a tight skull-like grimace, "or I will kill your small friend."

River tossed the revolver over with two fingers. One of the soldiers bent down to retrieve it. The others hurried to collect the scatterguns and other weapons from the unconscious crew.

Ranash stared down at the body of his dead officer. He kicked the corpse, making sure it was lifeless, and then drew his gaze back to River. The lenses on his eyepiece rotated, zeroing in on her. The breeze tousled his feathery white hair.

"You surprise me," he said. "You're the first people we've encountered who don't fear our magic."

"Magic?" River said. "It's not magic, it's technology."

"Yes, but do you understand it?"

"Of course!"

"I think not," said Ranash, "or you wouldn't have made the mistake of overcharging our capacitors and blowing up the weapons. If not for that, your plan may have worked."

He turned to one of the men next to him, a horrific creature with exposed metal ribs and a shiny silver jaw. "Kephir, round up these people and lock them in the cellars. Except for the woman, and the machine. When

I am ready, bring those two to my chambers... Take the rest of the bodies into the jungle. Burn them where the villagers won't see."

"Yes, Sergeant."

Chapter 19

A heavy fog boiled over the rim of Dragonwall, creeping down the mountainside, flooding across the stone terraces. Here and there fires glowed like dim halos up and down the wall. The air was thick with the scent of firewood, and down below, the gas lamps of Stormwatch were yellow orbs in an ocean of black that stretched to the horizon.

Kale stood beside the fire pit outside his living quarters, the mug of mulled wine in his hand forgotten as he gazed into the swirling flames. He heard low voices drifting out of the mist, the sounds little more than a muffled drone.

It had been three days since his return to Dragonwall. Three days without any word from Shayla; not so much as a hint as to whether she was even alive. He had gleaned a few clues about her disappearance, and had a few unconfirmed suspicions of his own. He had half a mind to grab one or two of the workmen while no one was looking, and have a talk with them. It wouldn't take a great deal of interrogation to learn the truth, he believed. And Kale had a good idea who to start with.

Unfortunately, as concerned as he was about Shayla, her disappearance was a relatively minor issue in relation to everything else going on. After meeting with the queen and sending out a handful of scouts, the reports that came back were disheartening: thousands of ghouls were amassing on the southern border. They had weapons and war machines, and they were *smart*.

They were not like the ghouls Kale had encountered in the past. These creatures were sentient. They had mechanically reinforced and enhanced bodies. This clockwork legion of undead warriors called themselves the Ana-nuit, which roughly translated as *the living,* or *the immortals*. And whatever they were planning, it wasn't good.

The few hundred militiamen and volunteers in Stormwatch didn't stand a chance against this army. Perhaps they could take refuge in the shelter of Dragonwall and wait out their enemies, but space and supplies were limited, and already refugees were pouring in from villages along the border. The kingdom simply didn't have the resources to house and protect so many.

Meanwhile, tensions continued to grow inside Dragonwall and among the populace of Stormwatch. Kale's position, having been granted by the queen, was tenuous. Not only was it a position that many felt he hadn't earned, there was also a feeling that Queen Aileen was herself not fit to rule. She was, after all, a woman. While the concept seemed foreign to Kale, it was deeply ingrained into their culture, and it was not something that he could change on a whim. He had learned enough about that from Socrates to know such a change could take decades, perhaps even centuries. For now, the people wanted a king, not a queen. One way or another, they were going to get one.

Kale had the option to suppress this rebellion, of course. A handful of beheadings would do the trick, at least for a while, until the rest of the knights and eventually the militia turned against him. This would happen inevitably. Then, he would be out of options.

His other choice was to marry Aileen. That was the surest way to silence their opposition and secure his position as First Knight... *Secure!* he thought, taking a sip from his mug as he stared into the flames. *I wouldn't just be commander, I would be king!*

The door to his chamber opened, interrupting his thoughts. Gavin called out his name.

"Outside," Kale called. "On the veranda."

His friend hurried across the room and stepped out onto the terrace. The elderly knight had shed his armor in favor of a heavy tunic and fur cloak. Kale noted that despite his lack of armor, Gavin still wore his broadsword and dagger on his belt. That wasn't surprising. Gavin was old for a knight, and he didn't get that way by being careless.

Kale offered his mug, but Gavin declined. "The scout I sent into the crater has returned," he said. "I thought you'd want to see him immediately."

"Bring him in."

Gavin put his fingers to his lips and let out a shrill whistle. A young man who had been waiting by the front door hurried through the room and out onto the terrace. He was dressed in dark clothing and a cloak, with a short sword strapped around his waist and a satchel over his shoulder. When he saw Kale, he snapped to attention.

"Commander!" he said, saluting.

"At ease," Kale said, with a wry grin. Through their training, the younger recruits were imbued with an admirable sense of discipline and formality. Strangely, these attributes seemed to disappear entirely as they moved up the ranks.

"Let's hear it, Wil," said Gavin.

"Yes, sir! I've been riding for three days, but I made my way through the crater, and-"

"Yes, yes," Kale said. "Did you find the train?"

"Aye."

"And you gave them the message?"

The scout hesitated.

"Come on," said Gavin. "Speak up!"

"I'm sorry, sir. The train was *wrecked.*"

Kale and Gavin exchanged a look. "You're sure? You're certain it was the Iron Horse?"

"Yes, sir. It was black with lots of brass pipes and chimneys."

Kale's face darkened. "What happened?"

"It looks like the Horse derailed, sir. The tracks were damaged, and it was lying on its side."

"And the crew?" said Kale.

"I'm sorry, sir. They were all dead."

Kale dropped his mug. The mulled wine splashed across his boots as he lunged forward, grabbing Wil by the lapels. "What did you see?" he said. "What *exactly* did you see?"

"I'm sorry, sir I went inside, and... the *smell.* There were bodies everywhere."

"Easy," Gavin said, putting a hand on Kale's shoulder. "Let him breathe. He's been riding hard for three days. Don't hurt the poor kid."

Kale released his grip and leaned back. He took a deep breath, trying to get control of himself. "Go on," he said after a moment.

"I couldn't stay long," Wil said. "The place was infested with dragons and other... *things.* I'm sorry," he apologized for what seemed like the thirteenth time. "They were all dead, sir. All of 'em."

"All right," Gavin said. "Go get yourself a meal. We'll summon you if we have any more questions."

Wil hurried out. Kale turned, staring into the flames. Gavin settled down on the bench across from him.

"She's dead," Kale said. "It doesn't seem... it doesn't seem possible."

"The blonde?" Gavin said. "I didn't know you were still pining-"

Kale glared at him, and Gavin bit his tongue. He lowered his gaze and stared at the fire.

"River and I grew up together," Kale said. "We were best friends. We fought the Vangars together..."

"She's gone to the gods now," said Gavin. "You have to let her go. She'll be waiting for you when it's your time."

"Are you sure?" Kale said, locking eyes with him.

Gavin sighed. "Let's go to the cellars. I know where there's a barrel with your name on it."

Kale shook his head. "Not right now. I need some time."

"I understand. I'll call on you in the morning. I'm sorry about your friends, but remember, their battle is over. *Pity is for the living.*"

Kale let the words slide off as Gavin quietly left. They didn't mean anything. No words could make sense of what had happened. The senselessness of it was staggering. It didn't seem possible that River could have died in such a futile and meaningless way. It didn't seem possible that she could have died at all. He had seen her survive so many things... things far worse than a simple accident.

They had battled against impossible odds together. They'd fought Vangars, defeated the Ancients, and escaped the Forgotten. Time and again, they had come through together. If only he'd known, he wouldn't have stayed behind...

Who was he kidding? She was the reason he *had* stayed behind. Somehow, Kale had thought he could prove something to River. He'd wanted to prove that he wasn't the irresponsible child she remembered; that he was a man, and she needed to take him seriously. It seemed so silly now. So trivial. Had he really thought he could make River love him?

The flames crackled, and an ember popped out. Kale stared at it as it hit the stones and slowly faded into blackness.

Chapter 20

After the failed attempt to overthrow the Ana-nuit, River found herself captive in a small stone building just a stone's throw from the pyramids. Socrates was there, but remained unconscious, and River was worried. She had already opened the hidden cavity in his torso to examine his internal mechanisms, and found everything working perfectly. River also knew how to open the secret locks that held the ape's skull together, but doing so would have been a waste of time. The automaton's head was filled with tiny intricate electrical parts that River couldn't possibly hope to understand. There were wires finer than a strand of hair, glass tubes filled with warm glowing light, and dozens of banks of memory circuits a thousand times more complicated than the electric motors and generators she had studied.

When River couldn't wake Socrates, she began studying the room, searching for some means of escape. It was sparsely furnished, with a crude wooden table with benches on either side. To the right stood an old pot-belly stove made of corroded copper and brass, and to the left, a small counter with a wash basin. Socrates was in the middle of the room, where they had left him sprawled out across the floor. It had taken half a dozen of Ranash's men to haul him there. The entire process would have been rather amusing, if not for the severity of their situation.

The building they were in had no windows, and two armed ghouls stood just outside, guarding the one door. The walls were made of impenetrable stone, but the roof was thatched straw, and the floor was made of lumber crudely laid out on the bare ground. River had already discerned her two most likely means of escape. The first and easiest would have been to climb the wall and cut an opening through the straw. The downside of this plan was that it would inevitably make a lot of noise, and even if River managed to get out, she would be standing on a rooftop in the middle of the village. And Socrates would still be trapped inside...

The second was to pull up the floor and tunnel under the wall. This was feasible, given enough time, but improbable since she had no tools and no way of knowing how long it would be before the guards returned. This plan also didn't take Socrates into account. Unconscious as he was, River wouldn't have been able to free him even if she could walk right out the front door. He was simply too heavy.

River heard a noise and her thoughts snapped back to the present. She glanced at Socrates, and realized that the fingers of his right hand were twitching. She rushed to him, kneeling down to take his hand.

"Socrates! Do you hear me? Wake up!"

His spine suddenly straightened, and his body went stiff as a board. Then his eyes opened wide and began flicking wildly from side to side, making loud *clicking* noises. They moved so fast that River worried something might break that she wouldn't be able to repair. This went on for about twenty seconds. Suddenly, Socrates went calm. He sat upright. His eyes came into focus, and he turned his head to look at River."

"Did it work?" he said.

"Not exactly."

At that moment, the door opened and one of the guards stepped inside. River realized they must have been listening at the door, waiting for Socrates to regain consciousness. This guard was more skeleton than corpse. His entire lower body was encased in a steel framework, and metal gears filled his abdomen. His upper torso was in slightly better condition, but only slightly. It was mystifying how the creature could still be alive. Just looking at it sent a cold chill down her spine.

It couldn't speak, but the ghoul made a gesture for them to follow. River glanced at Socrates, wondering if this might be the time to make their escape. Socrates could easily take out a couple of guards. But Socrates gave her a subtle shake of his head as he pushed to his feet and turned to face the guard.

"We will come without a fight," he said. "Please, lead the way."

River gave the ape a frustrated look, but Socrates ignored it.

It was early evening and the air was cool and filled with the scent of wildflowers and fermenting wine as they stepped outside. The stars twinkled brightly overhead, and torches flickered along the pathways and around the pyramids. It was an almost perfect evening, which made the appearance of the ghouls an even starker contrast to the paradisiacal setting.

The guard with the clockwork guts led the way and the other fell in behind. As they made their way down the path toward the great pyramid, River couldn't help second-guessing her companion's decision to cooperate with the ghouls. The guards were walking at a slow pace, focused more on watching their comrades who were gathering around a distant bonfire than on guarding their prisoners. The guard with the clockwork guts even stumbled, and barely caught himself before he sprawled out in front of them. The two were practically begging the prisoners to escape.

Perhaps, River thought, that was the reason Socrates had chosen to cooperate. Perhaps they *wanted* their prisoners to try to escape. Maybe they wanted to make an example of them.

The guards guided them around the great pyramid to a large tent that had been erected on the north lawn. It was not a sophisticated structure by any means, just simple linen draped across a framework of wooden poles. Compared to some of their other technologies, River was a little disappointed by the Ana-nuit's lack of creativity.

There were a few scattered bonfires in the area, where the undead had gathered to consume the harvest grapes, or to drink the wine, and two guards stood posted outside the tent's doorway.

River followed Socrates inside, and the guards stepped in behind them, flanking the doorway. The couple found themselves in a large room that made up the front section of the tent. A hanging linen curtain separated this room from the others, which River presumed were sleeping quarters. Sergeant Ranash sat at a desk with a large map spread out before him. To his left rested a bowl of grapes, and to the right sat a half-filled glass of wine next to an open bottle. He no longer wore the mechanical eyepiece, and had retrieved his hat, the overall effect of which made him look only slightly less horrifying.

The sergeant's long white hair rested like silver threads across the dark fabric of his sleeveless coat, and his mechanical arm made typewriter-like *clacking* noises as he used a brass mechanical pen to make a few notes on the map. After he finished, he set the pen aside, leaned back in his chair, and looked the couple up and down. His eyes were a dull blue color, and the organs seemed somehow shrunken inside the leathery folds of his flesh.

"I'm pleased to see that you're still functioning, Socrates. It would be a shame to lose a valuable commodity such as yourself."

"You overestimate me," Socrates said with a slight bow. "I'm no more valuable than any other machine."

The sergeant grinned, a horrific gesture that revealed rows of broken and misshapen teeth. "On the contrary. Humility is no virtue, machine. You are filled with valuable engineering information."

"We won't tell you anything!" River said, her lips curling into a snarl.

"Even so, I *will* learn what I want to know. Your humble mechanical friend will give up his secrets one piece at a time, if necessary. You will as well, should I choose to extract this information from you."

They were interrupted by a knock on the post outside. The clockwork guard pulled the flap aside, and another soldier stepped in. "Sergeant, we've taken inventory of the harvest. It's all accounted for. We even have an extra barrel or two."

"Excellent," said Ranash. "Tell the men they may drink tonight. Tomorrow, we'll load the wagons." The guard left with a bow.

Ranash took a drink of his wine. He didn't seem to swallow it so much as to savor it in his mouth until it had soaked into his palate. This, River realized, must be how the starfall nourished their brains. The liquid could permeate the ghouls' dry flesh, wicking through it and into the brain through a sort of capillary effect. No wonder these creatures could remain sentient, even as their bodies rotted away. She wondered how long it took until there was nothing left to keep alive...

Ranash, having finished his drink, turned his attention back to the captives. "Ah, now where were we?"

"I believe you were going to interrogate us," Socrates said.

"Why don't you just spare me the trouble," Ranash said, "and spare yourselves the pain? Tell me everything you know."

"Why would we do that?" River said.

"Because if you don't, I'll have your friends brought in here and flayed, one by one in front of you. I'll start with the little one. What was his name? Micah?"

River's hands clenched into fists. "If you touch him-"

"Easy," Socrates said in a low voice. "The sergeant is right. We should cooperate."

She spun around to face him. "What has gotten into you? I've never seen you like this before! Why should we cooperate with these monsters?"

"Hush!" the automaton said, glaring at her. "Remember your place, River!"

Her eyes widened, and her face reddened She opened her mouth to yell at him again, but found herself speechless. She clamped her mouth shut, crossed her arms over her chest, and refused to meet his gaze. Socrates turned his attention back to Ranash.

"Sergeant, I'm from a city known as Sanctuary. It is a place of high technology, similar to yours, but perhaps even more advanced."

"I see," said Ranash. "And in this city, there are others like you?"

"No, I am the only machine I know of with sentience. I was merely a complex toy -a mechanical distraction no smarter than your chariots- until an accident gave me self-awareness."

Ranash leaned forward, gazing into the ape's eyes. "You have my interest," he said. "Tell me more."

River began to protest again, but Socrates silenced her with a wave of his hand. "I presume you are familiar with starfall?"

The sergeant stared at him.

"Perhaps not," said the ape. "It is an element... like iron, or water. For some creatures, it is a necessary nutrient, for others a toxic hazard. Perhaps most relevant to you is the fact that this jungle is awash in the vital element."

The sergeant narrowed his eyes. "Relevant in what way?"

"I'm speaking of the grapevines, of course," said Socrates. "It was clear to me from the moment we arrived that this fruit somehow played a role in your unique... situation. Upon further investigation, I learned that the juice of the grape plays a pivotal role in the life and creation of the Ana-nuit. When I learned that these grapes were your sole source of nutrition, it became entirely obvious."

"Did it?" said Ranash. He seemed genuinely interested in the ape's analysis, but the unsettling tone of his voice belied this interest.

Ranash knew all of this, River realized. He was just prying, trying to find out exactly how much they had figured out. The sergeant took another drink of his wine, savoring the flavor, allowing its vitality to soak into the pores of his rotten flesh.

"...And what else have you learned?" he added with a dangerous glare.

"Oh, I know everything," said Socrates. "I know that the roots of the vine dig deep into the earth, where they gather starfall and filter it through the fine-mesh fibers of their pulp. I know that this highly filtered material enters the fruit in a purified and concentrated state that would be nearly impossible to replicate. And I know that without this purified juice, you and your kind would die."

The sergeant rose to his feet, glaring down at Socrates. When he rose to his full height, the top of his head nearly brushed the roof of the tent. River took an unconscious step back as the creature loomed over them. "You," he said, pointing a finger at the automaton, "will die for what you have revealed here today."

His words were slightly slurred, and he swayed unsteadily, as if he were drunk. The sergeant straightened his shoulders, trying to correct his balance. He shook his head, trying to shake out the dizziness.

"What is this? What's going on?"

"That would be my fault," Socrates said matter-of-factly. "I suspect it has something to do with the iron."

The sergeant licked his lips, making dry smacking noises. "What?"

"Iron," the ape repeated. "Another element, of which I'm sure you're aware, which is one of the most prevalent on this planet. In fact, much like the grapevine, it has the unique ability to attract and absorb large quantities of starfall."

The sergeant's knees wobbled unsteadily. He lowered himself back into his chair. "What did you do?"

They heard a thump, and turned to see that the soldiers who had been guarding the door were unconscious on the floor. The clockwork guts continued ticking, the machine steadily working away, unaware that its host was dying.

Socrates grinned. He reached into his vest pocket and pulled out a vial of fine black powder. He held it up in front of Ranash. The creature stared at it, confusion and fear mingling in his grotesque features.

"This is powdered iron," Socrates said. "I laced your fermentation tanks and wine barrels with it. It doesn't dissolve in liquids, of course, but when ground fine enough, it works as an adequate suspension."

Ranash tried to speak, but grunted instead. His voice rattled in his throat. "I don't understand," he managed to say. "What is happening to me?"

"Put simply, you're dying," Socrates said. "Although one could easily make the argument that you are already dead, and have been for a long time. That is a conundrum with which I must grapple in the future. I would not have chosen it thus, but I'm afraid you gave me no choice. I have poisoned you, Ranash. At this very moment, the iron is drawing the starfall from your body, leeching it from your organs and your flesh. Very soon, you will reach the critical juncture where your reanimated mind will no longer function. The rest of your men are dying, too. It won't be long now."

A panicked look came over the sergeant's face. He latched onto the sides of his armchair, trying to push to his feet. "Guards!" he shouted. "Guards, help me!"

He managed to move, he fell back, exhausted. His head lolled back against the chair and one arm dangled limply at his side. His hat toppled off, revealing the gleaming white of his skull. He reached out with his mechanical arm, his fingers clawing at the map on the desk. The paper curled, ripping as he clawed at it, pulling himself forward onto the desk. The wine bottle tipped over, crimson liquid splashing across the paper. The glass crashed to the floor.

"I'm sorry," Socrates said. "Violence is not my way, yet I find myself drawn into it time and again. I'm afraid I'm beginning to lose all faith in humanity. Or, perhaps I'm losing faith in myself."

"Guards!" Ranash cried out again, his voice hoarse and shaking with terror. The effort drained the last of his energy. He twisted awkwardly, the map crinkling and tearing beneath him as he collapsed across the desk. He let out a gurgling breath as he fixed Socrates and River with a menacing glare. "You will never defeat us," he coughed. "We... are... legion."

With this final exclamation, his body gave one last shudder and went limp. The couple stared at him, neither speaking, both waiting to see if he would recover. When, after a short time he hadn't moved, River had to ask: "Is he dead?"

"He's been dead for a long time," said Socrates. "Whatever it is -whatever makes up that spark of life that the starfall replaced inside of him- fled at the moment of death. The starfall kept his brain active, but clearly, there was no humanity left in this creature."

"This was your plan all along," she said, a look of understanding dawning on her face. "That's why you told me to cooperate with them. I'm sorry, Socrates. I should have trusted you."

"I would have told you sooner, if I could have," he said. "Their early arrival threw a wrench into my plans. Thankfully, I managed to get the important work done last night."

"You mean poisoning their wine?"

"Not just that," said Socrates. "I hope you don't mind; I borrowed your mechanical fairy."

"For what?"

"I programmed it to disperse powdered iron throughout the area. It has been flying since last night, scattering iron far and wide."

"You put iron on the ground?"

"Any ghoul that sets foot within miles of this place will immediately begin to leech starfall into the ore. It's not a permanent solution, of course, but it will do for now."

"Brilliant," River said. "Now I see what you meant by using their strengths against them."

Socrates grinned. He pulled back the tent flap and motioned for River to join him. "Shall we go release our crew from the cellars? I'm sure Thane is worried sick about you."

A meaningful glance passed between them, and River blushed. She wordlessly stepped past him into the cool night air.

Chapter 21

It was late, and Queen Aileen should have been in bed. Instead, she sat on the edge of the sofa, gazing into the great fireplace. Lately, it had been difficult to find sleep. The first few weeks after Dane's death had been a quiet time -a time of mourning, of introspection and reflection with her children- but lately she found herself more and more consumed by the anxieties and rigors of daily life.

She had a kingdom to maintain. There were taxes to be collected, salaries to be dispensed, decisions to be made. All of this was complicated by the fact that more and more, she found her subjects questioning her. There was a time when a man wouldn't have dared defy one of her orders. Now, they openly argued with her. Where men once averted their gaze respectfully, they now lingered, feeling her body with their eyes, whispering quiet jokes behind her back. She knew where it was all going.

Aileen had been planning her escape. The twins were young, but they were strong enough to travel. She might steal a carriage and make off in the middle of the night. She could take some valuables -the silverware, the goblets, the jewel-handled dagger made by Dane's great-grandfather- and sell these things off as necessary to buy their safety. The plan would work, she was sure of it. When the light of morning revealed her actions, Aileen and her children would already be miles away.

But she didn't know where she would go. She'd heard stories of other great kingdoms and cities. There was New Boston, a place of quiet sophistication and technological renaissance. There was Astatia, the young republic struggling through the aftermath of revolution and economic depression. It was a wild, free, vital place. The people were poor, but they had a wealth of spirit and courage. It seemed the sort of place she might make a new life for herself and her children.

Then there was Sanctuary, the almost legendary city deep in the frozen north. It was a place of high technology; a place of long-forgotten secrets and wonders that could bring tears to the eyes. The place had a dark and tragic past, and yet it had kindled the light of civilization at a time when it seemed a simple breeze might snuff it out entirely. Hidden in the libraries of Sanctuary were the keys to history, the records of times before the cataclysm, possibly even the answers to creation itself.

But Aileen couldn't choose. She only knew that she must go, and the sooner the better. The longer she stayed at Dragonwall, the greater the peril to her family. If only there were someone to guide her, to tell her which path to take…

A knock at the door brought her out of her thoughts. She glanced at the dagger on the table and dismissed it. If they had come for her, a dagger wouldn't do much good. If anything, it would probably hasten her demise. She went to the door and hesitated before pulling it open. What if this was it? What if they were waiting for her out there? What would happen to her children?

Summoning her courage, Aileen drew back the bar. As the door creaked open, she found herself face to face with Kale. The warrior's eyes were dark, his face a brooding mask. She could tell that something had happened to him -that he seemed somehow changed- but couldn't guess what that may have been.

"Is something wrong?" she said, gazing up at him.

"May I come in?"

Aileen stepped aside with a welcoming gesture. Kale brushed past her, storming into the room. He stared into the fireplace as she barred the door behind him.

"What happened?" she said. "What is this darkness you bring into my chambers?"

Aileen approached him. She stood before him, taking his hands in hers and gazing up into his face. "Please, tell me what's wrong. You carry a storm on your shoulders. I worry for you."

"I worry for all of us," Kale said. "I don't know that the army at our border can be stopped. I know we can't fight them without proper leadership, but I fear that your people will turn against you."

"Then we will flee," Aileen said. "We'll take a carriage in the middle of the night-"

"No, there is nowhere we could go. Nowhere they couldn't find us. And could you leave them so easily? I don't believe you could. It would haunt you, knowing that you had abandoned your people in the time of their greatest need."

Aileen reached up to brush his dark bangs away from his smoldering blue eyes. Her hand lingered there, the backs of her fingers caressing the scar on his cheek. She flattened her palm against it, feeling the coarseness against her skin.

"Speak to me, my friend. Tell me what I must do, for I am lost. I see the gathering storm, but have nowhere to turn."

Kale took a deep breath. "I know what you must do," he said. "I've tried to deny it, but now I see that all along there was no choice."

She narrowed her eyebrows. "Kale, what are you saying?"

"I'll do it," he said. "I will marry you, and you will make me your king. It is the only way."

Her eyes widened. "Do you mean it? Are you truly willing to do this? Don't toy with me. I am already a broken woman. I don't think I could survive a jest like this."

"It is no joke," Kale said, drawing her into him. "We will marry. We will unite the kingdom, and then we will have the strength to fight back the horde."

"Yes," she said, collapsing into him. "We must." Then, as a thought occurred to her, she pulled away. Aileen squeezed her eyebrows together in a look of undisguised anguish. "No, I can't do it. I can't force you into this... it would be wrong."

"You're not forcing me," Kale said in a quiet, reassuring voice. "I'm doing what I should have a long time ago. I want to do this. I'm not a child anymore, and it's time I stopped acting like one."

Aileen sighed as the weight of the world slid from her shoulders. She pressed into him. A smile came to her lips. "My king," she breathed, pulling his face down towards hers. "Kiss me, my king..."

Chapter 22

The crew of the Iron Horse met little resistance from the Ana-nuit soldiers. Even those who had not yet partaken of the grapes or the wine had been affected by the iron-laced soil. Even in miniscule amounts, this cumulative loss of starfall was catastrophically damaging to their systems. Many had already fallen to the ground in a semi-conscious or unconscious state by the time River and Socrates left the sergeant's tent. Those soldiers who still had the strength to stand were like drunks, staggering through the village in a state of confusion. When the villagers sensed this weakness in their masters, they fell upon the Ana-nuit and slew them.

Socrates and River found the rest of the crew locked in one of the wine cellars, and together they spent the rest of the night gathering the soldiers' bodies and burning them. The villager known as Grandfather helped explain what had happened to the others, and how it was that they were now free, but their reactions were subdued.

River had expected rejoicing from them, or at least some thanks, but neither were forthcoming. She couldn't hide her disappointment. She spoke of this to Socrates later, when they were alone. After having restored the pyramid's power source to its original configuration, the pair stood on the upper level, looking out over the village.

"Look at them," she said. "They're no happier today than they were yesterday. They're free now, but all they can think to do is to keep harvesting."

"They don't know how to be free," Socrates explained. "These people were born into slavery, told what to do and what to think from the moment they were born. They have been conditioned not to think for themselves, but always to do what was expected of them."

"It's tragic," River said. "Do you think they'll ever understand? Will they be able to survive?"

Socrates shifted, and the gears inside his body made *clicking* noises as they meshed together, compensating for the change in balance. "It will be some time before they truly comprehend what freedom means. The great tragedy is that these people have no values or culture of their own. This has been stolen from them by the Ana-nuit. Now, they will have to start at the beginning. They will have to decide what things will be important to them, what belief systems they will adhere to, what gods they will worship. They must build their culture from nothing."

"Why don't we just tell them about the beliefs we've encountered so far? They can choose what to believe, and forget the rest."

"It would be easy for us to do so, but it wouldn't be fair to them," said the ape. "These people have a right to form their own opinions and set their own standards. Anything less, and they would still be slaves. Without chains, of course, but slaves nonetheless. They should be free to form their own values and opinions without outside interference. When the time comes, they will venture beyond the safety of their village and their pyramids. They will observe and interact with other cultures, and by then, they will have the discrimination they now lack."

"Let's just hope they don't turn out like the Ana-nuit," River said with a sigh. "I'd hate to go through this all again."

Before leaving that morning, Socrates and River went to say their farewells to Grandfather and the others. A large number of villagers had gathered around the old man, seeking his advice. This proved a perfect opportunity for Socrates to thank everyone and wish them well before leaving. Strangely, as Grandfather translated the ape's words, a clamor arose among the villagers. Socrates waited as they argued in loud voices, until at last Grandfather turned to face him.

"They warn you not to leave," the old man said. "They say it is dangerous to leave the crater. In the Firelands, you will only find more Ana-nuit, and they say there are other creatures, even worse."

"Tell them we thank them for their concern," said Socrates, "and assure them that we will be just fine. Now that we know what to expect from the Ana-nuit, we will be prepared."

The villagers did not seem consoled by this information, but Socrates would not change his mind on the matter. After this, the crew returned to the Iron Horse.

A short while later, Socrates blew the train's steam whistle and released the brakes. The chassis moaned like a ship on the high seas as the steam engine went to work. A rush of pure white vapor came out of the exhaust pipes, and the wheels made loud whining noises as they began to roll.

By this time, River was already back in Engineering. She had taken Grandfather's warning to heart. If they were to encounter any more ghouls on their journey, she wanted to be prepared. It was with this in mind that River sat down at the engineering table and began sketching out designs for scatterguns, grenades, and bombs that might be used as delivery devices for powdered iron. Considering the inherent softness of the raw metal, this would prove a unique challenge. A scattergun, for example, would have to operate with a smaller powder charge than usual. Same with a cannon. And a bomb? Socrates wanted one, but River wasn't even sure it was possible…

As she worked, night fell, and the jungle outside her windows turned black except for the occasional flash of deep green foliage in the train's lights. The engineering compartment was quiet, the air thick with the scent of old grease and sulfur. River leaned over her worktable, taking measurements and doing calculations by the light of a single lantern. Little did she know that a few hundred miles to the north, Kale and Aileen were working on plans of their own:

It would take a few weeks to plan the wedding, but in order to pacify the citizens of Danaise, the couple had decided to announce their marriage immediately. This would be enough to stop the revolt and secure Kale's position. He wouldn't be king yet, but nobody would have the courage to challenge him. Not with Aileen's commitment made public, and the entire kingdom watching.

In the meanwhile, Kale was doing his best to stop thinking about River. He had loved her -yes, he could readily admit to that- but she was gone now. She had gone to the next world without him. It was a cruel trick of fate, her dying in that way, but there was nothing to do but accept what he could not change. Perhaps Kale would meet River in the afterlife, and be able to tell her all the things he had always wanted to, but for now, it was time to stop acting like a child and start living up to his responsibilities: Protecting the kingdom, saving thousands of lives... that he *could* do. That was his new priority. It had to be.

Kale accepted this new lot in life with his shoulders thrown back and his head held high. If any regrets brought a pang to his heart, he would bury them deep inside and do his best to forget. This was his life now. It was the right thing to do. He would wed Aileen, unite the kingdom behind his banner, and prepare the militia to repel the coming invasion.

This was what worried Kale most. The warrior had seen the legion with his own eyes. He knew what was coming, and everything else paled in comparison. He wasn't even sure defeating them was possible. That was why he had sent word to New Boston, Astatia, and even Sanctuary. If ever there was a time for the kingdoms to unite, it was now. The question was, could they do it in time? If not, he might be joining River in the next world sooner than he expected...

Epilogue:

Two thousand miles to the west, River's mother had a few problems of her own:

"It's my orchard!" Britch Farmer shouted as he jabbed a thick, soil-stained finger under the nose of his neighbor Jym Walker. "You had no right to cut my trees." Britch's nearly bald head was practically glowing with fury, the smooth skin shining in the light of the courtroom's flickering lanterns.

"Hogwash!" exclaimed his tall, lanky neighbor. "Judge, Mr. Farmer started moving his fence line the moment the Vangars left. He planted half a dozen trees on my property, and he's stealing all the water from the creek. My cattle need that water! I demand he be held responsible."

The Honorable Breeze Tinkerman let out an audible sigh. It was late. She was tired. She no longer had the patience to try to appear interested in the petty bickering of the two incompetent farmers. She'd been listening to it all day, all week, all month... it seemed the bickering and backbiting never ended. If it wasn't farmers, it was the cobbler who shared a wall with a baker, or the schoolmistress who shared a lot with the blacksmith. Someone always had something to complain about, and for some reason rather than figuring it out on their own like adults, they all felt the need to resort to the law.

Why? She simply couldn't understand it. In most cases, the best a judge could do was to make sure *no one* came out happy. When it came to establishing a principle of fairness, that was usually the best measure. They all knew it. Very few people ever left the courtroom with smiles on their faces, and yet they just kept coming, day after day.

Breeze glanced at the papers on her desk, studying them over the rims of her reading glasses. The deed to the land, she observed, was less than a year old, but the map hadn't changed in a century. Somehow, she suspected the complaints hadn't either.

"Is this true?" Breeze said, looking Britch up and down. "Have you planted trees across the property line?"

Britch hesitated. He glanced at Jym and then drew his gaze to the bench. He couldn't quite meet the judge's stare. "It's impossible to say for sure. There's no way to know exactly where the property line is."

Breeze frowned down at him. "According to this survey map, the property line cuts through the middle of Washback Creek. Hasn't it always been so?"

"But the creek moves!" Britch protested. "It's farther left this year. That makes it mine, don' t it?"

"Not when you're stealing my property!" hollered Jym.

Breeze shushed them, and the two immediately complied. They knew better than to upset her. They'd done it before.

Breeze tapped the end of her pen on her lower lip. It was almost impossible to believe that less than two years ago, these two men had been slaves without any property whatsoever, and lucky just to be alive. It was confounding, the idea that after living through that, these men would stand in her courtroom arguing about whether the property line should be five feet to the left or the right. She had half a mind to throw them out of her courtroom. The only thing that kept her from doing so was the knowledge that they'd be right back the next day, starting the argument all over again.

Breeze was about to speak when the doors at the front of the courtroom burst open and a messenger came rushing in. It was a young man in his early twenties, wearing a heavy coat and scarf and a pair of goggles pushed up over his forehead.

"Apologies, your honor," he said as he jogged across the courtroom. He threw open the gate and ran to the bench, holding a letter up in the air. "I have urgent news from the capital."

Breeze accepted the letter. She examined the wax seal, which was official and fully intact, and then opened the envelope. She spent a few seconds scanning the page. When she was done, she lowered her head to stare at the messenger over her glasses.

"Will you be sending a response?" he said.

"That won't be necessary. You may leave."

The young man nodded and went rushing out the way he had come. Breeze put the letter aside, and turned her attention back to the two men standing before her. She looked them up and down for few moments before dipping her pen into the inkpot. She started scribbling. When she was done, she held up the survey map so both could see it.

"Gentlemen, I have stipulated that from this day forward, the property line will run in a straight north-south line through the center of the creek as it sits now, and regardless of where it may relocate in the future. The boundary is permanent. As far as I'm concerned,

Washback Creek can turn around and run straight up into the Blackrocks. It won't make a lick of difference. The property line does not move, ever. And as far as water rights, you both have the right to irrigate or supply livestock. Nothing more. If I catch you extracting more than your fair share from that creek, I'll lock you both up until you can't remember your own names. Do you understand?"

"But my orchard!" exclaimed Britch Farmer. "If the creek moves, he'll steal the water, sure as the world, if you let him."

"Bah! That's my grazing land," said Jym Walker. "If the creek moves west, my cattle will starve and this fool will be planting orchards as far as the eye can see."

"Then I recommend the two of you spend more time reinforcing the banks to make sure the creek stays right where it is, and less time arguing with each other." They began to protest, but Breeze leaned forward, glaring at them, and they fell silent. "Keep this in mind," she continued, pointing her gavel at them. "This is the third time in a year the two of you have been in my courtroom. If I see you again on this matter, at least one of you is going to *lose* his land. Maybe both of you. The state can always use a new federal waterway. Do I make myself clear?"

They mumbled their acceptance, and Breeze brought down the gavel with a *bang!* that woke the bailiff in the corner. He bolted upright, knocking over the stool he'd been napping on.

"Sorry, your honor," he said. "It got so late…"

"Never mind, Jasper. See these men out, and lock the front doors behind you, if you please."

"Yes, your honor. I'll see you in the morning."

"Good night, Jasper."

The sound of the old bailiff's boot heels echoed in the courtroom as he led the men outside. They shuffled out and began arguing the instant their feet hit the street. The voices quickly faded, but Breeze waited until she heard the key in the lock before she leaned back in her chair and took a deep breath -the first full breath she'd had since lunch.

She rose from the bench, gathered up her lantern, and headed into the back room. There, in the mudroom, she removed her black robe and hung it on the hook by the door. She glanced at the clock on the shelf above the sideboard. The gears made a quiet *click-click-click* as the pendulum swung. The waning moon face was resting on its side, with its eyes closed and its pointy nose sticking straight up towards midnight. It was eight p.m. already. Where had the time gone?

Breeze stoked the fire in the old potbelly stove and started a pot of water for tea. She was hungry, but she didn't feel like cooking. There wasn't much in the pantry, anyway. A crusty loaf of stale bread and some moldy cheese did not sound promising. Maybe she would go out for dinner. The blossoming young town of Fern Hollow was brimming with new inns and restaurants that she was eager to try. But not yet. First she needed to rest, and to clear her head. It had been a long day.

Breeze climbed the stairs to her bedroom, where she took a moment to adjust the chimney flue, making sure the room would be warm at bedtime. Through the second-story window, she saw light snow falling on the street outside. The streetlamps threw off dim halos in the storm, and fountains of steam gushed up from the sewer grates in the cobbled street. The buildings of

Fern Hollow stretched into the distance, their lights glittering in the frosty winter air.

It was a beautiful view, and a heartening one considering that this had all been wild prairie land just a few years earlier. Slowly but surely, Astatia was looking less like a wild frontier and more like a real country. A country that, by morning, would be covered in a blanket of white.

The harvest was finished, thankfully. Winter had come early to Astatia this year, and more than one farmer had nearly lost his crops. One week earlier and they would have been heading into winter with empty granaries and crops frozen in the fields...

The teapot gave out a shrill whistle, and Breeze hurried downstairs. When she entered the kitchen, she failed to notice the shadowy figure by the doorway. It was only when she heard the ominous *ka-chunk* of a heavy metal footstep behind her, that she wheeled around brandishing a long kitchen knife.

"Long day?" said a man's gravelly voice.

Breeze placed the knife on the counter and exhaled a long, deep breath. "You nearly stopped my heart. I don't think I'll ever get used to that sound."

The tall, shadow-covered figure hung his coat on a hook by the door and stepped into the kitchen. His left foot made that heavy thumping noise on the floorboards again as he moved, and his left arm made quiet *whist-click, whist-click* sounds as he approached her.

"Tea?" Breeze offered, pulling a second cup from the shelf.

"Just a little," the man said. "I haven't eaten yet." He settled onto a chair, and the legs creaked under his weight. The light of the lantern gleamed on the shiny brass plate on the left side of his head, and his mechanical eye *buzzed* as the lenses adjusted their focus.

Breeze joined him at the table. "I thought I might go down to the Steamwhistle Inn. I hear they have seafood flown in fresh every day."

The old man raised his eyebrows. "I'm surprised they can afford to do that. Most of our planes are out of commission now, except for a few gyrocopters."

"I know. Soon, we'll have nothing left but balloons. It's tragic in a way. I feel like we're moving backwards. We accomplished so much... learned so much in such a short amount of time. But now that the Blackrock steel is all gone..."

"Maybe this is nature's way of pushing back; telling us we moved too fast."

"Perhaps." She sipped her tea and then stared at the steam rising from the hot liquid. "Still, I can't help feeling like everything's falling apart."

He smiled gently, reaching across the table with his mostly-mechanical left arm. What flesh remained was badly scarred. The gears *whirred* and the fingers made clicking noises as Breeze squeezed them in her hand.

"What's bothering you?" he said. "This is about more than an orchard, or that broken down old plane out back."

"I got a letter from the senate today."

"More refugees?"

She nodded. "Ten thousand Kanters crossed the border this week alone. Giants, plainsmen, Riverfolk. They're all moving north. I don't know what we'll do with them all. We barely have the food to feed ourselves, and we expect half a million more by spring.

They've overrun South Bronwyr, and Avenston has had to call in the militia. The people are already on the verge of starving, and now these idiot senators want to send more refugees here. Here! How will we feed them? Where will they live? In tents, in the snow? I don't know what we'll do, old friend."

He gave her hand a light squeeze. "We'll do what we have to," he said, his good eye sparkling in the lamplight. "We'll do what's right."

Breeze smiled, blinking back the frustrated tears brimming her eyes. "I know I can always trust your guidance, Tinker. What would I do without you?"

"No matter," he said with a wide grin. "I know what you'll do *with me*. Let's go get some dinner."

The End

Look for the next installment in the *Iron Horse* series, available soon at Amazon.com and other retailers!

A note from the author:

Thanks for reading "Clockwork Legion." I hope you enjoyed this book. I'm grateful for the opportunity to share my work with you, and for your support. Your review at Goodreads, Amazon, or your favorite bookseller's website would be extremely helpful and very much appreciated. While sharing your valuable feedback, your reviews help me, and help other readers to find my books.

Made in the USA
San Bernardino, CA
10 February 2017